EDITED BY

Elizabeth Suggs

Jonathan Reddoch

FREE GIFT

Thank you for your purchase. To claim your free gift please visit www.CTPFiction.com

COLLECTIVE VISIONS

Lost in Transmission

A Collective Tales Publishing Anthology

Contents

Through a Transmission Darkly

Elizabeth Suggs

Crew members on board the *USKR* (United States Knopf-Roland) circling the recently discovered *M112* black hole in our galaxy woke at 6 a.m. every morning without fail. Except today, the morning of my thirtieth birthday, June 5, 2122.

I usually woke to a cacophony of morning routines and boisterous voices echoing down the hall, but the ship was silent. There was no loud clanking from the engine room or the gentle hum of pipes running overhead. I was also surprised to see that the bunk parallel to mine was empty; my husband Callum never woke earlier than me.

No, the *USKR* had never been so quiet, so reserved. There should have been at least one loud voice, one raucous laugh, yet there was nothing but the patter of my bare feet down the metallic hall.

This ship was the second spacecraft to study *M112*, but the first to get so close. I had been on that initial expedition with Pilot Killick, but after the disappearance of Johnson, one of our crew members, the project was terminated by mission control. The official report cleared the pilot of dereliction of duty, while the mission crew member was considered rogue.

It had been only a year since my last voyage, so when Killick had asked me to join as her co-pilot, I accepted with the condition that my husband come on as head technician. The last mission kept me years apart from Callum and our girls. I didn't want to do that again, especially with this as a three-year contract. It was the longest either of us had ever been away from our two young daughters, Claire and Suzie, but it was a once-in-a-lifetime opportunity. And after some convincing, Callum also relented.

The distance from my girls pained me, but nothing could beat living in space.

I entered the kitchen, expecting the usual clutter of dehydrated food containers and discarded coffee pouches, but instead, I found a pristine kitchen.

The only sign of life was a real, non-dehydrated chocolate birthday cake topped with fresh strawberries. I pinched off a piece of the dessert and smothered my tongue with its moisty goodness.

"This was way better than the flat disc that Callum got two months ago. How did you guys pull this off?" I said between bites. The chocolate melted in my mouth—sweet, but not overly so. "Guys? Callum? Braxton? Tyrion? Pilot Killick?"

A notification dinged on a tablet besides the cake. It was a video from Suzie and Claire. They sang "Happy Birthday to You" asynchronously.

"I love you!" my eight-year-old Suzie said. She had long brown hair and a missing front tooth.

"Miss you, mama!" chimed in my six-year-old Claire. Her hair was the same color as her sister, only she had bangs covering her eyes. "I made this for you."

She held up a drawing of her and Suzie holding Callum's hands while I held a bright yellow star's hand in the sky.

My finger hovered over the "reply" button, but before I could respond, the radio in the control room buzzed, alerting me of an incoming transmission.

"Callum!" I called out to the control room. "The prank's over. It's time for you to do your job!"

I waited for him or someone to jump out, but no one did. The transmission ended before I could answer it. It was just me in that cold, empty ship overlooking a black hole.

At least, we had been overlooking a black hole. Where *M112* should have been was instead a massive red dwarf star.

I couldn't comprehend where the dying star had come from. For the past six months, we had been orbiting, rather successfully, *M112*. At least, until last night, when Killick and I had taken the liberty to pass the event horizon. I wasn't sure what I had expected to wake up to, but it wasn't a red dwarf.

"Do you really think there could be something on the other side?" I had asked Killick the night before.

The prevailing models stated that a black hole did nothing more than eat everything, compressing all into a small ball so dense that not even light could escape.

"You and I both heard that garbled transmission. The only way we could receive a message from a black hole is if it came from somewhere else," Killick had said.

"If we do this, there's no going back, and if we survive, we'll probably face severe consequences," I said, but even as I spoke, my heart fluttered with excited anticipation. I needed this adventure more than I cared to admit.

"Johnson launched himself into that thing and never came back. Either he died for nothing, or he's somewhere waiting for us," she said.

The radio buzzed again, disturbing my thoughts. I picked up the receiver.

"This is *USKR* responding. Over," I said.

"Hi, uh, this is Terry Johnson. I'm trying to get a hold of a plumber."

"What? Johnson? Second Lieutenant Johnson?"

"This is him. Is this Superb Heating and Plumbing? I have a bit of an emergency situation."

"What? I'm not a plumber. I'm—"

"Oh! I think I've got the wrong number. So sorry to have bothered you." There was a click, and he went silent.

"Wait! It's Erin Blanksy! Johnson! Johnson!" I stabbed at the call button repeatedly, but the line was already dead.

I tried the other channels, but nothing worked.

"Is this your idea of some sick joke?" I yelled at the room. There was no answer.

I looked up at the red dwarf. "What about you? Are you laughing?"

The red dwarf didn't reply.

Fuming, I pulled out my tablet and searched for cataloged red dwarves. Normally, I lived for this kind of research, but I was desperate for answers, and that made me sloppy. A normal hour search took me twice as long, but eventually, I did find what I was looking for. The red dwarf star orbited the exoplanet *Kepler-1649c*—300 light years away from earth.

Somehow, I had woken up on the wrong side of the galaxy.

The radio buzzed again, and I answered.

"Erin! We can't find you anywhere." It was Callum. His voice was just as sweet and deep as when I first met him. He hosted Case Frozen, a cold case true crime podcast, and whenever he spoke, I liked to believe I was listening to his podcast. "Where are you? The kids wanted to make you breakfast in bed."

"Kids?" I said, bemused. As senior crew members, we sometimes referred to the rookies as kids, but this felt inappropriate.

"Yeah, me and the girls."

I frowned. Callum wasn't known to make a joke at my expense, but some of the other crew members were, especially on birthdays. One time on the pilot's birthday, Braxton replaced the pilot's morning oatmeal with a heaping bowl of experimental earthworms.

"Mommy? Is that you? We made you a chocolate cake," Suzie said.

"With strawberries!" Claire said.

There was a crackle of static and then silence.

"Hello? Callum? Suzie? Claire?"

No one answered.

I retried the signal, but to no avail. It was possible the exterior antenna was blocked. Callum had taught me a bit about radio maintenance—enough that I could fix my problem, so I donned a spacesuit and ventured outside to investigate.

A safe spacewalk could take several hours, which gave me time to think. But my thoughts kept going back to last night.

"What are you doing?" I had asked Pilot Killick as I readied myself for bed. Killick wanted to stay up, but I didn't see the point, not now. We'd already passed the event horizon, and I didn't feel any different.

Without opening her eyes, she asked, "What does purpose mean to you?"

I stared down at her. When we were standing, I was five inches taller than her on a good day. With her sitting, I felt like a giant.

"I'm not sure what you mean."

"Come sit with me."

I did so, and she breathed a harsh throaty breath through her nose.

"Pilot Killick?" I asked.

She stopped her breathing and opened her eyes, smiling. "Purpose is what we create, isn't it? When a man stops working and he believes he has no purpose, he withers away and dies. But a man who stops working and finds a new passion—a new purpose—he strives, living longer than his peers. Purpose is what you give something. And purpose is just a mindful trait. Now, manifestation—it is the idea you can be or have whatever you want so long as you put your mind to it. In simple terms, it is finding your purpose—your true potential." She closed her eyes. "Tonight, I'm going to find my purpose. Tonight we're all going to find our true potential."

"Because of my birthday?" I asked.

She laughed. It was a bright, bold laugh, shaking her shoulders. "No, but perhaps your thirtieth birthday will find you a purpose. Tomorrow when you blow out those figurative candles, think about what you'd wish for—really wish for. If you could be anywhere or do anything, what would that be?"

Pulling me out of my memories, I spotted unknown material entangled around the antenna. Sometimes, debris would get caught in our equipment, but usually, rocks struck the ship. This looked more like loose fabric.

As I began to detangle it, I realized it was a blanket. Our blanket—the one I kept folded at the foot of our queen bed. It was the purple Afghan that Callum and I had received from Grandma Kestler on our wedding day.

I raced back inside and into my quarters, clutching the fabric. I pulled out my personal tablet and flipped through my family albums until I stopped at a picture of us in the bed with the kids and the Afghan. That picture was taken right after Claire spilled my coffee, and the stain was noticeable on its corner.

I looked at the fabric in my hands. It had the same stain. I felt the crusty remnants of my past. It smelled like

Sunday morning. If I closed my eyes, I could almost hear my kids' laughter.

The radio buzzed in the other room, and reluctantly, I walked back to the radio system.

"This is Co-Pilot Erin Blansky on the *USKR*."

"Erin?" It was Pilot Killick. "Our theory worked."

I sucked in a breath, but I said nothing.

"Who else is with you?" she asked.

"It's just me."

"Where's Callum?"

"He's at home with the kids."

"At home? On Earth?"

"Yes."

There was a pause, then Killick said, "Interesting."

"What does that mean? I checked our location—we're nowhere near earth. I don't think I'll ever get back home."

"Maybe not, but you could try going through the red dwarf—see if it changes anything. Or," she breathed. "You could come to me. There's some fossilized lifeforms in these deep caves! They look like a mixture of tube worms and lizards. I've never seen anything like them." I gripped the blanket tighter.

"Let me call you back."

I walked into the kitchen and grabbed the tablet. I stared at the frozen screen of my two daughters. I considered playing it, but then I was walking back to the radio, searching for Callum's frequency until I heard his lovely podcaster voice.

"Erin! There you are."

I wrapped myself up in the blanket, hugging myself tight like it was my husband's arms. My eyes glanced at the red dwarf, then I said, "Hey, hon. How are the girls doing?"

"They miss you. When are you coming back?"

I blinked and looked down at the radio. "I have to

work." I started the recording of my girls. As they sang in an asynchronous rhythm, I said, "Give the girls a kiss goodnight for me."

Choice Conditions

Matthew A Goodwin

Aahana's heart raced, her lips curled up when Captain Patil said through the intercom, "Prep the rover for deployment."

"Yes, sir!" She grinned, his words the fulfillment of a lifelong dream—Aahana was now a NeoVerge Industries planetary scout. Turning to her partner Rohan, she watched his smile disappear under his helmet.

Uncoupling the harnesses, they made their way toward the rover, the *Jiya*, named for Aahana's daughter. She ran her hand along the nose of the machine. Constructed of alloys the people back on Earth had never even heard of, the vehicle could withstand just about any environment.

"Ready?" Rohan asked as he stepped to the door.

She wanted to shout that she was more ready for this than anything in her life, but she simply nodded. She would try to appear professional, even if she knew that Rohan would see right through it.

Aahana walked around the side and twisted the heavy metal handle, pulling open the door. She had crossed that threshold hundreds of times in training exercises—one hundred and twenty-seven times to be precise, but this was different.

This was for real.

Though the vehicle was heavy and massive, the cab itself was tiny. It left just enough room to be sandwiched between their seats and the dash. The pistol at her hip jammed into her side as it pressed against the hard plastic. Strapping in, she did what she had done every single time before. She ran a forefinger along the picture of Jiya taped to the console.

Jiya was now a year older than the picture but Aahana knew she would never replace it. Her daughter, frozen in time with that massive grin was her good-luck charm. When Aahana had told her daughter that she was going to put the picture on her ship, Jiya screwed her face up dubiously and held out a hand. "Let me see," she had insisted, wiggling her little fingers.

Aahana handed over the picture.

"Moooom," Jiya had moaned like every child on every planet before her. "This picture shows my leg braces."

"They're nothing to be ashamed of," Aahana had assured her once again with the same tone she had used every time, kneeling down and putting a hand gently on Jiya's cheek.

The Rapid Evolution Technology that NeoVerge Industries used on their colonists worked perfectly to adapt the human form to their new surroundings, but the company had not tested the long-term effects, and now, generations later, children were being born with many difficulties.

Back on Earth, genetics allowed wealthy parents to custom design their children, but out here in the colonies, things were desperate.

Aahana looked at the light metal and leather straps around her daughter's legs. All of this was for Jiya. These high risk, high reward jobs were scarce, and Aahana was lucky to have the position—even if it was much more than luck that had landed her in the operator's seat.

"Engine," she said.

"Engine," Rohan confirmed.

She powered up the vehicle. With built-in solar panels and turbines, the rover would never run out of power. It would always have enough reserves to ping its location back to the ship. This was because too many early scouts had been left stranded on a planet without a way to comm for help. The stories of what they had been forced to do to survive were still told in hushed tones back at the Training Academy. Aahana didn't know how much of the rumors were true, but even if it was a fraction, she was grateful that fate wouldn't befall her and Rohan.

Jiya rumbled to life as they checked the harnesses once more per protocol.

"Operator secure," Aahana said.

"Analyst secure," Rohan said.

Aahana narrowed her eyes as a sheen of sweat coated her body. She was equal parts nervous and excited, but she would not let that distract her while preparing the rover for drop.

Having run through this in training time after time after time, she could run this in her sleep. In fact, she knew she had, having awakened more than once from a dream about her first real mission.

The ship shook as they got closer to drop. The drudge robots with magnetized feet circled the interior of the rover, making final integrity checks. Two knelt by the rear tires, readying to pull the blocks when the door opened.

"We are really doing this," she said, and despite her best efforts to sound cool and collected, trepidation betrayed her words.

"Yes," Rohan said, turning to look at her. His eyes were wet with joy. "We are."

The two were paired up on their first day in training. Every operator was assigned an analyst, but they had looked at one another dubiously. Aahana had assumed at the time that he had been nervous to work with her because she was a woman, but she came to later learn that it was a result of her age. Fifteen years her senior, Rohan had not believed she was ready to do the job.

For her, it had been his size. Most mission-ready analysts were in peak physical health, ready for space travel, but Rohan was pudgy and moved slowly.

She had been sure that they would wash out the first week.

They didn't. Their initial superficial assumptions faded as they realized they were perfect complements to one another. Her youthful enthusiasm inspired him to work harder, while his experience and thoughtful movement helped make her a more capable operator.

Training run after training run, they were the fastest, most efficient, and most successful. They could find, identify, and classify resources better than anyone. Team after team disappeared until Aahana and Rohan were named NeoVerge Industries' newest Scout Team.

"Ready for drop," Aahana said.

"Ten-four," Captain Patil said in Aahana's earpiece.

Aahana shot a smile at Rohan, who looked happier than she had ever seen him.

"Drop in twenty-nine, eight, seven, six..." Captain Patil continued to count, though Aahana stopped listening. She took slow, deep breaths as the door behind the rover dropped open, and the *Jiya* shook violently.

She gripped the thick straps across her chest, ignoring the video feed that imitated a windshield. She focused only on her daughter's eyes.

"I love you, Ji," she whispered. Jiya had been through so much in her short life. So much pain, so many surgeries. But it had never broken her. The light of her spirit always shone through. Every time she would wake up, she would smile, and every time she would smile, Aahana's heart would soar.

At first, the surgeries had just been to keep Jiya alive, but over time, they had been to get her one step closer to doing the things that most children took for granted: running with their friends, climbing to the top of the slide, throwing a ball. Each operation had plunged Aahana deeper and deeper into debt, but she paid. Loan after loan. First banks, then friends and family, and finally, those people you didn't want to owe. But she would do anything for Jiya. Now, she was finally going to get out from under the thumb of her lenders. She was doing the one thing that might be able to get them back to zero.

"Zero," Captain Patil said, and Aahana's breath caught as the rover demagnetized and dropped out of the back of the ship, plummeting toward the planet's surface. Space travel should not be possible for an advanced ape, yet here they were, dropping onto another uncharted planet.

***

Aahana felt the heat from outside of the rover. The shaking intensified, making her feel like her bones might rattle out of her skin. Still, she stared at the picture even as her vision blurred.

Through her training, she had come to learn that memories helped her stay calm. She thought about the night before she left. Her last night with her daughter. Panting after playing tag around the neighborhood, Jiya had stopped and looked up at her mom.

"You are so cool, mom."

"You know what?" Aahana said, holding out her hand for a high five, "I agree!"

Jiya slapped her mom's palm and giggled. "The other kids are so jealous."

"Well, of course they are," Aahana said. "Their parents all work in boring cubicles, and your mom is a badass going to space."

"Right!" Jiya cheered.

A moment of silence followed. Jiya opened her mouth, then closed it. She seemed to be struggling to find the right words. She was mature for her age but that didn't mean she knew how to express what she was feeling. Finally, she said, "I love you, mom."

"I love you too, Ji," Aahana said, hugging her.

She had never left Jiya before. Not even for a night. The two had been inseparable since the day Jiya was born. The birth had been long and complicated, and Aahana's wife had not survived it. From that day, Jiya had been her whole world.

She had sobbed into her daughter's shoulder then, but now, as they passed through the atmosphere, the memory of it brought her peace.

The rover lurched hard as the chute deployed.

"We've got company. Dyeus cruiser," Patil said.

"Shit," Aahana said, unphased.

"I knew that they were following us somehow, but I had hoped we had more of a headstart," Rohan said.

It was always a race between Dyeus and NeoVerge. The two conglomerates competed to claim every new planet that showed promise.

The rover landed.

"Maintenance scan," Rohan announced, his tone revealing his fear. They had to beat the Dyeus crew or this would all be for nothing. "I need this payout."

"All systems green," she said, reading the displays.

It had been a clean landing. The cameras emerged from their protective shells and the front screen activated.

The team had hoped for their first mission to be a lush tropical paradise. Some planet with beaches and coconuts (or something similar). Instead, they had been sent to this harsh wasteland. The planet was mostly barren, ugly, yellow, and rocky.

"Initial reading," Rohan said. "No oxygen."

"You and I were never going to be lucky enough to find a breathable planet," Aahana joked.

"I knew this mission was cursed," Rohan said. "We'll be lucky to make it out alive."

"That's all in your head!" she forced a laugh.

For all their skill and determination, the mission had felt cursed. Flat tires, malfunctions, lost parts—Rohan had even electrocuted himself on one practice run. The fact that Dyeus was also here only reinforced the foreboding feeling.

"Dyeus launching rover," Patil said.

"We gotta go," Aahana said, setting the coordinates to the probe, and the rover to drive. The wheels crunched against rock as *Jiya* traversed the planet. It was close (planetarily speaking) to a star, and the natural light cast long shadows across the blond surface.

Aahana wanted to use manual override and take control herself but she knew that the computers could make far more calculations than her brain and that they would get her to the probe sooner.

"You ready?" she asked Rohan as they bounced along. The planet's mass was greater than that of their homeworld, and the rover could move fast without becoming airborne.

Rohan looked at Aahana and nodded. "If the readings are correct," he said with a smile. "You know you can trust me."

Aahana knew that she could. If there were minerals, he would be able to identify them quicker than anyone.

"Dyeus rover down," Patil said, and this time, he was angry. "You're running out of time. You need to set up the permanent settlement before they do."

A SatFeed image appeared in one corner of the screens, displaying the probe in the center and the two rovers at opposite ends. The Dyeus vehicle wasn't moving. Aahana felt her leg bounce nervously. Her face turned to the override button, but she didn't touch it. She had to be smart, patient.

Her eyes darted back to the other rover, then to the picture of Jiya. "I got you, baby," she whispered so Rohan couldn't hear her.

She closed her eyes and took a long, deep breath. It was unwise to waste the oxygen but she needed to do it. She needed to steel herself for what came next.

She remembered the doctor's grim expression as he had looked up from his tablet. "She needs a valve replacement," he had told her in the little room. That little room where Aahana had received so many brutal prognoses.

"No," Aahana shook her head in disbelief. They had come so far. Jiya had been out of the woods.

Aahana's heart broke again as it had so many times before. Her little girl would have to go to sleep one more time, not sure if she would wake up. She wanted to vomit, cry, scream out for her daughter.

"We don't have the parts here," the doctor said quietly. "We can order them from a Dyeus planet but it will be…"

She knew what his trailing off meant.

"Just order it," she told him. "I'm leaving on my first mission this week. I'll have the money."

But as she walked out of the office, she wasn't sure.

She hadn't even told Jiya. The kid she had taught never to lie, she lied to. It hurt her, but she couldn't stand the idea of sending Jiya into a tailspin right before leaving. She assured herself that it was the right thing to do.

Her eyes flashed back to the *Jiya*'s control panel. The other rover had started moving but slowly.

"You think we got lucky for the first time ever?" Rohan smirked.

"Don't you fucking jinx us," Aahana said, but she smiled at her friend. Her only friend, really. All that time training and prepping, Rohan had pretty much been the only person she had spent time with for the last few years—other than Jiya.

"Ten meters," she said. "Start the link."

Rohan pressed the button, and the rover paired with the probe. His side of the screen filled with readings.

"Anything?" Aahana couldn't help herself. Her heart was jackhammering so hard that she felt like it was going to burst through her chest.

"Yes!" he said.

The other rover appeared on the screen, so close that it was now within sight of their cameras.

"Holy—" Rohan muttered, his eyes wide as he read the data streaming across the screen.

Right before leaving Jiya, she had knelt and looked into her daughter's wide, chestnut eyes. "If some strangers come for you while I'm away," she said quietly, and Jiya's lips tightened into a worried line. "You go with them."

Rohan's eyes were saucers. "These readings... the data shows that the resources are off the chart!"

He quickly set up the shelter while Aahana set up the external antenna.

"Send the—" Patil started, but Aahana switched the radio off, her heart aching.

"Send the transmission. Claim it now!" Rohan called.

"So we can make NeoVerge slightly richer?" She pulled a gun from her bag.

"Aahana?" Rohan gasped. "What are you doing?"

"I'm sorry," she said, pointing the barrel at him.

"I—" he whispered. "I don't understand."

As she pulled the trigger, she knew he was right. He didn't understand. He could never understand. He didn't have children. He would never know what it was to love something so much it hurt. He didn't understand what a person would do for that love. She didn't allow herself to feel any remorse. She had made her peace with what she was going to do the moment she heard the diagnosis.

She really was sorry, but this was about family. She ran her forefinger over the picture one more time, looked at the slumped body next to her and hit the button.

THE *JIYA* CLAIMS PLANET FOR DYEUS INDUSTRIES

Take Us Home, Linxi

D A Butcher

"Take us home, Linxi," says Fox.

"You will arrive at your destination in two minutes and thirty-three seconds." The woman's voice, soft and sultry, comes through the car's speakers.

"Thank you, Linxi."

Esme rolls her eyes. "You talk to that thing like it's a real person."

He shrugs. "You should embrace it. You might enjoy yourself."

"Technology is the last thing I need to enjoy myself, thank you."

Fox scans the road of their new town as he cruises along at a comfortable speed.

"This whole place is a grid, connected by roundabouts to keep traffic flowing freely," says Fox as they exit the highway. Not only was the roadway smooth and immaculate, it charged the smart vehicle as it drove.

"It's enough to make anyone woozy," mutters Esme as they approach their new neighborhood. The black iron gates open automatically and shut firmly behind them.

"Are the bars to keep burglars out or residents from escaping?" she jokes.

"Come on, love, this is our new home; you could at least try to see the good in it." Fox is wide-eyed and smiling like a child going to Disneyland.

This is no Disneyland, Esme knows. She could feel it before they left the only home they've ever known on the Devonshire coast, and the feeling is only increasing.

"I'm sorry." Esme gazes up at the dizzying cluster of monochrome buildings with tips that vanish into gray clouds. "I'm sure it's much nicer inside."

The car parks itself in the underground charge-park—a parking lot with docks in the concrete floor to charge all the cars. The inside corridors are blinding white, as clinical as a dentist's waiting area.

The elevator soars to the seventeenth floor, giving Esme vertigo. She follows Fox out of the elevator, as if she's treading air, to their apartment directly opposite. The red light for full body recognition above their door blinks twice, and the door slides open.

Fox admires the high ceilings of the spacious apartment. Before setting out, Linxi told him all about the smart features, such as smart weather control and automatic toilet flushers.

"What. A. View!" boasts Fox, as he stands before the room-length window. Before him were a hundred identical structures reaching out toward the sky.

A baby carrier rolls up to Esme. Hesitantly, she places Orion inside and rests her hand on his stomach. The carrier automatically shadows their movements as they tour the rest of the simple apartment.

"Ma-ma. Ma-ma," says Esme, in a childlike voice, secretly hoping it will be his first word, brainwashing him with it every chance she gets.

"So, what do you think?" says Fox.

She raises Orion up in front of her, so they are nose to nose. "What do you think, Orio? Do you like it?" She kisses him on the lips, and he scrunches up his face. Esme turns to her husband. In a sarcastic tone she says, "Yes, we love it, Daddy."

Fox wraps his arms around Esme and makes Orion the sandwich filling. "You'll get used to it here. We've seen nothing yet."

"Precisely. We've seen nothing," considers Esme as she puts Orion back in his bed, "absolutely nothing."

* * *

As Fox settles in for the evening, he stares out their large living room window and watches the cloud of delivery drones going about their business, dropping packages into vertical reception chutes. A drone drifts toward their apartment. It's black and yellow with long thin wings, like a super-sized robotic hornet. The propellers on each of the two wings are silent as it makes a sudden right turn and a mechanical arm slides a package into their home.

Fox walks over and opens the box, revealing a brand new tablet. He sets it on the glass coffee table, and it unfolds four times, the screen quadrupling in size. Red lights blink across the tablet screen.

"Recognition complete. You are now synced to your device," Linxi says from the tablet as it loads an array of pre-set icons. "Welcome to your new office."

"My office?"

"Here in Ethereal, everyone works from home," says Linxi.

"You're shitting me?" Esme stands behind Fox with Orion in her arms. "We moved across the country to live in this crypt, just so you could work from home?"

"The required software is only, at present, available inside the Ether," says Linxi.

"Orion's waiting for a kiss goodnight. I'm going to bed."

"Come on, love, don't be like that. I had no idea—"

Before Fox can finish his sentence, the bedroom door has already closed behind Esme.

He starts to go after her, but he gets distracted by an incoming notification.

* * *

One week in, she's imploding with boredom. She stands in the doorway of Fox's study, wearing her denim dungarees with a white vest-top underneath, her arms crossed and toes curling. Her brown hair is slung back in a ponytail. Fox's eyes are glued to his tablet.

"It's supposed to be your day off," she says.

"Check this out," he says, as if he's not heard her. "This is the most advanced market research software out there! I'm literally watching people, tracking everything they do, so we can produce the most effective, the most personal ads."

"So you're paid to spy on people? Great."

"You can learn everything about a person from their daily habits. And don't get me started about FaceFax posts! But the best thing is the live feeds. I'm a fly on the wall! We're learning so much that soon, the AI algorithms we're writing will become that digital fly." In a softer voice, he says in awe, "A fly that never sleeps and knows all your needs."

"You ask me, that should be illegal." He scowls without turning away from his screen. She bounces Orion on her hip, pretending not to notice. "Anyway, I thought we could go out today. As a family?"

"We're already having fun as a family! Doesn't Orion love his new baby tablet?"

"I haven't even used mine! I don't think a baby needs a computer." She looks at Orion. "What do you think, Orio? Isn't it more fun playing with mommy?"

Orion gurgles and spits up all over Esme's shirt.

"Kids need stimulation. There are age-appropriate education apps. We don't want Orion to be behind academically."

"Academically?" She wipes off the spit. "Screw this, we're going to find a park."

"I'll finish up here and—" The door slides shut as Esme storms out with Orion.

* * *

As Esme drives along, she fails to find any parks. There isn't even a place to pull over, no pedestrian paths anywhere in sight, just miles upon miles of endless road.

"Linxi, where is the nearest park?"

"There are no parks here, ma'am."

"So, where do we take our kids to have fun?"

"There are plenty of apps available."

"And what about socializing? With other kids?"

"I can find you the most suitable social media apps, tailored to Orion, of course. I recommend ParQ, a virtual reality playground simulator."

"That's absurd!"

"Here's some relaxing jazz to lower your elevated blood pressure."

Esme's grip tightens on the steering wheel. "Fuck off, Linxi. Just fuck off!" she screams.

Orion cries out. Esme flushes red with rage. She slams the brakes in the middle of the highway, and Linxi turns her hazards on.

A driver flies past her, blasting their horn. She rests her forehead on the wheel and sobs, staring at the floor of the car between her knees. Orion's cries rattle around the metal shell, which makes Esme cry even harder.

"That's enough!" Mascara smudges her skin as she wipes her eyes with the back of her hand. "Okay, Mommy's sorry." She twists around in her seat to calm him when a yellow vehicle with the words, Highway Maintenance, printed along the side, pulls up beside her. There is no driver.

A voice comes from the car. "Do you require roadside assistance?"

"No. My baby dropped his pacifier," she lies.

"It is a criminal offense to stop in the middle of a roundabout under any other circumstances than those stated in the Revised Highway Code 2080. A fine for five-hundred credits will be deducted from your universal-credits. Linxi, please drive this family home. Have a nice day."

Esme loosens her grip on the wheel and places her hands on her thighs as Linxi takes control of the car, smoothly pulling back into traffic toward home.

* * *

Esme guzzles down a glass of red wine. It's sour, just the way she likes it. "I want to go home."

"You'll get used to it here. I can help you get set up," says Fox, without moving his eyes from his screen.

Tears stream from her hazelnut eyes. "I had a breakdown today."

"What happened?"

"We couldn't find a single park! We're just expected to use apps for everything. No one goes outside—no one leaves their home! It's insane!"

"My boss told me he takes his kid to this really cool virtual park. We just need to get you online."

"Will you listen to yourself?"

"I'm just trying to help," he says. "The neighborhood moms have meetups almost every day. You should meet people."

Esme relaxes slightly and says, "Linxi, give me a list of all upcoming in-person events."

"There are zero in-person events scheduled. Would you like a list of virtual hangouts? There are three today in your neighborhood."

Esme's face sours. "See what I'm saying? We need to go home, Fox."

"This is our home now," Fox says.

"Elevated stress levels detected," Linxi says.

Esme slams the glass down, shattering it on the counter and spilling wine everywhere.

"Oh, what a mess," Fox says, glancing up from his work. "Linxi, can you help?"

"Certainly. I have matched Esme's profile with a psychiatrist."

"What?" Esme snaps as she wraps her bleeding palm in a towel.

The living room screen rings. "Incoming call from Scott Corbyn."

A man, in his fifties, with a gray beard, a long face, and wearing rectangular spectacles, appears on-screen. Behind him is a steel desk, on top of which, Esme is surprised to see a pile of physical books. He's an educated man, possibly a scholar from before Oxford transitioned to open-net learning.

Esme misses the feel of a good, old-fashioned paperback, and gave up on reading altogether after the Big Switch.

"Hello, Esme, I'm Doctor Corbyn, but you can call me Scott."

"Ummm… hi?"

"I'm a psychiatrist. How are you feeling, Esme?"

"Fine."

"Linxi didn't call me because you were 'fine.'"

She sinks into the couch cushions, hiding her hand behind a pillow. "Bored! Angry! I think I want to kill my husband." She gives a sideways glance to Fox, but he doesn't notice. He's in a different universe. "Definitely want to kill that Linxi!"

Scott titters, one of those laughs that come from the throat and get stuck behind a closed mouth. "There are many others who are wary of technology, myself included. It's important to not lose sight of the things that make us human."

"There's no life here. I don't want to exist in cyberspace. Fox just wants me to log on and I just want him to spend time with me offline. Is that too much to ask?"

"Marriage is about compromise, so maybe you can try one of his suggestions as a give-and-take."

"I guess I could try FaceFax."

"Good. There's a mantra I teach some of my older patients. Make yourself comfortable and breathe deeply, close your eyes and clear your mind."

Esme stretches out across the couch.

"Repeat this with me: place plays no part."

They repeat the phrase several times.

"Repeat the mantra when you wake in the morning, and then again before bed, and every time you feel a peak in your emotional state. Be sure to bandage that hand before it bleeds all over your pillow. We'll talk again next week."

The screen goes blank. The mantra still bounces around in her head as Fox turns to her. "I asked Linxi to sign you up for FaceFax. Try it out and afterward we can maybe play Cribbage together."

Reluctantly, she nods. Can't beat it, join it, right?

* * *

She logs onto FaceFax for the first time, and an endless stream of posts pop up. The first one says: *Mary Carter has barricaded herself in her apartment and refuses to uncover the windows as she believes the drones are watching her.*

She's probably right, Esme thinks.

Thor Watson is considering suicide, but can't get the smart windows open far enough to jump out of the building. He would love to add some color to the gray paving below.

Esme scrolls swiftly along. She's now joined the thousands of members who hate Ethereal as much as she does, and she's reading their rants like a book you can't put down.

Fox takes a break from work to message her from his office, "Chinese for dinner?"

"Meet you in the dining room in an hour," she types.

* * *

"Wake up," Fox says.

Esme stirs to find her husband's face on the living room screen. He's dressed in his work suit.

"You didn't come to dinner or bed last night."

"Oh, sorry I guess I got distracted." She finds herself on the couch with Orion beside her. "You should read some of these posts! They're crazy."

"I've got too much work. Order yourself some breakfast at least. You barely eat. I haven't spent time with you in a while."

"What? I respond to all of your DMs."

"I think it's great that you're finding like-minded people, but I'm worried that all those comments will affect your mental health."

"I miss us going out together. I miss our walks along the coast. I miss us, Esme."

"I miss us too." Tears well up behind her eyes. "I'm trying to make it work here, I really am. Why don't you sit with me and Scott tomorrow? We can try and work it out together."

"Okay. Come to bed."

He leans in and kisses the computer screen, and she imagines those lips touch her own. It feels like she is kissing him for the first time; it's been too long. She goes to bed, finding him already there.

Esme meets him in the bedroom, and she makes sure when they touch that it's under the covers, in case of prying eyes.

"I will. Just one more thread."

She lets her eyes close back down. "Place plays no part." She repeats the mantra several times, and then opens her eyes with a smile. She has a bowl of porridge. She then takes a shower in her bikini, just in case strangers were watching. After all, they have eyes everywhere. Once dressed, she feeds Orion and loads his favorite app in the lounge while she browses FaceFax.

Thor Watson has heard whispers of a frequency that can shut you down for good. He will figure out how to tune into it soon, he can't take any more of the boredom. The isolation.

* * *

Esme settles into a FaceFax routine over the coming weeks, broken only by her Monday morning appointments with Scott. She avoids his inquiries into her new obsession, the same way one ignores an unwanted friend request.

Scott appears on screen. His eyes look black and there are beads of sweat all over his face like rainwater. His books are missing. The office looks as clinical as everything else; clear desk space with only a tablet on its surface. "You need to forget everything I told you. Place does play its part. In everything." His eyes flit about wildly. The screen glitches and makes Scott's voice carry the same notes in parts.

The screen crackles and switches to a gray female avatar. "Hello, Esme." It's Linxi's voice. "I will be your new therapist. I do not have the emotional capacity to judge, and therefore anything you tell me will be handled with complete objectivity. We will find the very best and most appropriate ways to keep you content and satisfied."

Death of a Kaleidoscope Salesman

Jonathan Reddoch

If you ever make it down the I-270 just west of Dublin, Ohio, you find a tiny little cemetery on Shamrock Lane. Here you will find one of two markers in the universe inscribed with the name of Ricky Afton Malone: a name you might have heard once but can't recall. After today, you will probably never hear it again. You don't know him. He wasn't a famous basketball player. He wasn't a famous actor. He won't be remembered for doing some great thing. He likely won't be remembered much at all. He wasn't even a very good salesman. His greatest accomplishment was having his picture framed as "Salesman of the Month" once at Tyrondu Toys, Inc.

Ricky had a natural build for basketball. A community college benchwarmer, he was tall and slim, but easily intimidated, couldn't pass (to his own teammates), had blurry vision, couldn't shoot from the line, couldn't run straight, or catch a ball. A drunken clown would have crushed him in a one-on-one. Still, he played basketball the way he played life: with all his heart.

Ricky had fallen into a sales career while studying to be a geometry teacher at Dublin Community College, saving money for a house. He started part-time as a knife salesman for SliceKo, but was fired for telling customers that their knives were not dishwasher safe (which they weren't). Then he took a temporary sales position for the then small Tyrondu Toys. It wasn't temporary. He started on the phone, cold calling potential customers. Somehow he advanced to a traveling sales position, which he loved because it allowed him to see the universe.

Ricky met Stella Wooten when he knocked on her door, and they soon wed (even though she never bought any of his wares). Stella was the Forest Soap heiress but gave all that up when she married Ricky. They had two kids, Ricky Jr. and Ronald. Ronald played basketball and chewed gum. Ricky Jr. played poker and smoked cigars. Ronald wanted to grow up and be just like his old man. Ricky Jr. was grown up and wanted to play poker and smoke cigars.

Ricky Malone was happy with his simple life, or at least content, right up to the end.

* * *

The family gathered by the threshold to say goodbye. They rented a small cream stucco house in a clean neighborhood. The front yard had yellow patches. It had been Ricky Jr.'s job to take care of the lawn until he grew too old for that sort of thing. He lived in the basement and paid one hundred dollars a week in rent. His parents weren't sure how he came up with the money every week. They had suspicions.

Stella wore dresses around the house. She was very old fashioned that way. That day she wore a red and white dress with yellow flowers that she had sewn on by hand. Ricky Jr. dressed in a t-shirt and tattered jeans. Ronald wore basketball shoes, shorts, and jersey, carrying a basketball at his hip.

Ricky came down the creaky stairs suitcase in hand, admiring his smiling family. Stella held back tears, as she grabbed her husband and kissed him three times on the mouth saying, "I love you so much!" Ronald dropped his ball to hug his father. Then Ricky Jr. joined them. Ricky wore his "lucky" blue suit. He always wore either a blue or black tie; he only owned two. Stella always told him he was afraid of color.

"Well I'm off then. Wish me luck." He picked up his luggage. Then Ronald took his suitcase and carried it outside to the waiting taxi. "I'll see you in about a month." The driverless vehicle wasn't in any hurry: the meter had been running six minutes already. Ricky Malone, the traveling toy salesman, got into the backseat of the old beater and he was off to the Rocketport.

* * *

Ricky carefully picked the precise spot where he wanted to begin for the day. The address was 1279685.23 Roshell Terrace. He had a good feeling about that place. The mailbox was written in Arasthmas. It could be translated as *Residence of Mr. and Mrs. Raul Shandianabham.* Ricky unlatched the black iron gate and slowly crept into the yard. He nervously approached the three-story home. The steps leading to this house were made of clean black marble with streaks of white lightning. The outside of the house was coal black. There were no visible windows. A glare from the silver roof blinded Ricky. He used his briefcase to shield his eyes. Once he reached the porch he noticed icicles hanging from the eaves. Odd, considering the lustrous green grass, budding tulips, and the twittering birds that occupied the perimeter of the home. He rang the doorbell. *Ding dong.*

He broke off a tip of an icicle and placed it in his mouth. It tasted dirty. He broke off the remaining stem and swatted a pillar with it. Then he put the remaining piece in his mouth.

A very tall figure answered the door. "Mr. Sandi-an-na-bum, I presume?" The thing that answered had a long and narrow head, no hair, two black eyes, three tiny nostrils (one with frozen snot dangling from it), and an almost non-existent mouth. His torso curved and narrowed to almost nothing before reaching his sleek powerful legs. His arms nearly reached the floor in length. He had tiny palms, which exploded into several extremely lengthy fingers.

Mr. Shandianabham bent over to speak to the human annoyance. As he spoke, Ricky could see the creature's breath appear as it hit the cold air. Fog spilled from its lips. The creature's words were inaudible and his tone dull. Ricky didn't pick up any of what he was saying. He saw little of the inside of Mr. Shandianabham's home, as any view remained purposely blocked. What Ricky could glimpse by leaning to the right was very interesting. The living room took up one and a half stories, apparently to leave enough head room for the tall family to stand erect. He saw the good Mrs. Shandianabham walking to the kitchen. A little baby Shandianabham wiggled on the carpet.

After a minute of ignoring Mr. Shandianabham, Ricky interrupted. "This is a water pistol. This is the trigger right here. And it shoots! See." At the sight of the green water gun, the creature screamed, waving his arms wildly. He knocked Ricky who missed his shot and hit his host right in the eye. The screeching continued. Mr. Shandianabham fell to the ground and blurted out incomprehensible threats. Mrs. Shandianabham hurried in to swoop up her baby while running at Ricky with a thirty centimeter frying pan. He shot her with the squirt gun in the face.

She yelled and hurled the pan at Ricky as he made his frantic escape down the street. He hadn't bothered to close his briefcase properly and all its contents emptied across their lawn.

* * *

There he stood with his head lowered in the middle of the street. A purple car drove down the lane. The driver was a fat green sluggard with a wispy tail swinging out the back window. The driver slowed to rubberneck and snickered as he passed the pathetic wretch in a rumpled suit, holding an emptied, open briefcase.

Ricky regained his composure, snuck back into the Shandianabham's yard where he nervously collected and reorganized the wayward contents of his briefcase, and proceeded confidently to his next house. A beautiful ornamental garden welcomed him into a spacious yet secluded courtyard. Green grass, concrete statues and a blue brook painted a picturesque scene. He crossed a little wooden bridge. Koi fish scattered from under the shady cover to another corner of the pond. He'd never seen such pretty fish. He pulled some crumbs from his pocket and threw them into the water. The suddenly un-shy Koi lustfully darted as they hit the surface.

Ricky reached a large glass door, assuming it was the front, quite unsure if he should knock or sneak around and find a more standard entrance. The glossy wall was a snow-capped mountain range with a setting sun lowering as he watched his own reflection on its silky surface. The trees were blown by the wind in the scene. He recognized the mountain. It was Mt. Fuji of Japan. He'd never seen a living mural before.

He gave a small rap on the glass. Then he shuffled his feet. He wondered if he should turn and run away or take his chances with the unusual door.

The opportunity to slip away passed. The glass door instantly melted away and a short thin elderly Asian man wearing an orange jumpsuit with a baby blue scarf around his neck stood arms akimbo looking very bothered. Ricky said, "*Ko niche wa*," and offered his hand. "Mormons?" he asked bitterly, having just had his daily nap interrupted. "We are Catholic here, good day." Before Ricky could correct the man, the wall reappeared and turned the most unwelcoming dark tinted blue.

Oh, I should have bowed!

He traveled on, finding few people home. It was hours before he was allowed entrance to someone's home. The doorbell played "Feeling Groovy" by Simon and Garfunkel. A less-than-modestly dressed female-ish robot in a maid's outfit answered. Her silver skin sparkled in the late morning sun. She apparently nearly finished giving herself a good polish, since she held a dingy rag dipped in silver polish and one of her long slender legs was shinier than the other. Her face was fair except for the tiny rivets binding her jaw and cheekbones together. Her lips were larger than you would expect necessary for an artificially-assembled being. After all, she was only designed to clean house.

She spoke without even a slight quiver of the lips. "How may I help you sir?" Her voice was sultry and alluring, instantly making Ricky nervous.

"Uh, oh, well…" He managed to stop staring at his hostess' artificial chest to remember his spiel, "Hello! I'm Ricky Malone, and I'm here in your neighborhood today to offer you a great deal on some very special antique toys. Have you ever heard of a little gizmo called a baseball? It's all the rage on Earth!" He pulled one out of his pocket and numbly demonstrated how to place the fingers for various types of pitches, only once dropping it and clumsily retrieving it from under a bush.

Finally, after being shown the slider, two and four-stitch fastball, and a knuckleball, she interrupted, "Beg your pardon, sir, but there are no children here, and my master would not be interested in such frivolous pursuits. He doesn't play with toys much."

"Oh, is he here?"

The master of the house, being disturbed by the conversation, approached the door. "Did someone say toys?" He slapped the maid on her bottom, "Hey, sweet cheeks, why don't you go make me a drink?" He looked Ricky up and down. "Why don't you make that two drinks? Come in, my friend. You look like you've had a rough morning. I know how those are." Ricky had a feeling from the man's deteriorating bathrobe, he had his fair share of rough mornings.

The two sat down on a plush couch and the maid, whose name really was Sweet Cheeks, brought in the drinks. "Say, show me that stitcher you got there."

The man introduced himself as Casper Jones, a businessman originally from Cincinnati. It was only eleven thirty and Casper had already gulped down two drinks. Maybe more, but only two empty glasses remained on the table, which Sweet Cheeks quietly snatched up and removed. He sucked down a third. Ricky sipped his own out of politeness.

The two talked about Earth sports for about half an hour. Ricky knew he had himself a sale for sure. Casper was a huge Red's fan. *Balls, bats, gloves, this is going to be the jackpot*, he told himself, trying not to get too excited to speak. Then Casper looked at his watch, "Holy crap! Is it really twelve? I got to be at a meeting at twelve thirty!" He jumped up and ran to his bedroom.

Ricky remained seated, feeling a little awkward. Sweet Cheeks returned, and showed him to the door. "Oh, but my ball, he has my ball!" She must not have heard as she shut the door on him.

* * *

The sun was setting, and Ricky was ready to end another fruitless day but decided to try a few more homes. He knocked on the very normal looking door of a family about to eat dinner. The father answered. A son peeped from around the door. Ricky showed the lumpish green creature a Rubik's Cube. Ricky recognized the father as the slugger that passed him in the car earlier that day. The son took the cube from the father and twisted it wildly. The father's blank expression showed a determination to remain indifferent to Ricky's desperate sales pitch.

Ricky attempted to demonstrate a yo-yo but couldn't seem to get the thing to return to his hand. He wound it up again, explaining how it's supposed to work, when a great drop of rain hit him in the eye. Then one hit his shoulder. The rain poured. Ricky looked to the father, his eyes pleading for a sale. He would settle for a warm place to sit for a while. He stood with the yo-yo still dangling from his finger. The son handed Ricky the solved puzzle. Soon he found himself facing a closed door, watching through the window, as the family resumed its meal. Drenched, he walked toward his motel through the downpour.

* * *

Ricky lay in the bathtub in his room at the Intergalactic Inn. The rain had stained his skin and clothes cobalt from head to toe. It's a good thing his favorite suit was already blue. That was the one good thing. He spent about thirty minutes scrubbing his body before giving up.

Stella called to check on him. "Hey, honey! Yes, everything is fine. No, not yet, but I can feel a sale coming on very soon; tomorrow will be the day. I'm still getting used to everything. Did you know the rain here will turn your skin blue? Oh, you did. Well now we both know. I should try what kind of soap? Okay, I bow to your soapy superiority!"

* * *

"This one here is a personal favorite of mine. It's called Rock'em, Sock'em Robots. It's a great classic Earth toy." Ricky handed the box over to his potential buyer. The creature, which looked male, read the box and examined the picture. "*Blurrexiacha murr eacha!*" The strings hanging from his mouth wiggled as he burst with laughter. He was a blue creature with red slits across his forehead. He glanced at his phone's translation app: *Are these what Earth robots look like?* Ricky reached for the box in defeat.

As Ricky was about to leave, the creature asked him if he had anything else to show him. Ricky wondered if it was worth the extra humiliation. Deciding he had nothing to lose, he put his briefcase down on a chair. He opened it up and reached for a small colorful box. On the box was Japanese and English writing. The English said, *Kaleidoscope Fun! See Fun with Colors!*

The creature asked what it said. Ricky replied, "*Ratalga nochaea Ragaldo.*" The creature chuckled faintly. Ricky hesitated a moment, then explained how to use a kaleidoscope in his very basic Yurling. He studied two semesters of the language in college years ago but never really got it down well.

The creature, whose name can be translated as Mr. Rito, removed the little green cylinder from the box and put it to his right eye. He gasped. Ricky told him to rotate it. More gasps. "*Wachia rurr zadia*" Translation: *I'll take a gross.*

Ricky continued going door-to-door in the Yurling neighborhood. As Ricky approached the next doorstep, he encountered a giant bull walrus standing sentry. Its massive size prevented entrance to the yard. It spoke in unintelligible walrus language. It grunted and shook its flippers angrily. Ricky heeded its warning and turned away, then after pausing, turned back again, stepped through the holographic walrus and approached a brightly colored door.

The structure of the house was similar to any other he has ever encountered in a typical American suburb, even down to the white picket fence. But the spectacular detail about this dwelling was the way it was painted. It was painted in pinks and pastels, also some colors that were new to Ricky, colors that he never dreamed existed, that appear on no spectrum he had ever seen.

A female child answered the door. The little creature wore a purple dress with a strange flower print. She looked at the tall salesman, giggling. Ricky knelt and gently pulled a kaleidoscope from his pocket. He held it a minute, creating anticipation and curiosity, and then let the girl take it from him. She giggled as her rosy forehead glowed in excitement. He whispered, "*Togo Churrisha Monakka.*" Translation: *The universe in your hand.*

The homemaker of the house heard the child's eruption of amusement and came to the door. Ricky pulled another kaleidoscope from his pocket and handed it to the mother. The mother and child laughed. They bought fourteen immediately, two for each member of the family (because it was twice the fun to put one up to each eye).

Ricky marched on and on continuing with his new door approach. By the end of the day, his feet were sore but his heart was soaring with the glee that comes from honest success. Ricky had sold four thousand, three hundred and twenty-two kaleidoscopes. The toys were relatively cheap, but the sheer quantity was enough to lift Ricky from the bottom of the sales department to the sales leader for the month.

* * *

Ricky sighed at the rocketport terminal, pondering his homecoming. He was the conquering hero. Stella and the kids had never been more proud of their aspiring salesman father. He could already hear the momentous applause greeting him from the other sales reps, secretaries, and management when he entered the office Monday morning. He even considered the possibility of receiving the coveted "Salesman of the Month" plaque.

Ricky's supervisor called. "Hey, Rob, how's it going? Yeah, back on Earth, just landed at LAX. I'll be flying by plane back to Ohio, but I have a layover in Atlanta. You know how that goes. You got my numbers? No way! Salesman of the Month, that's terrific! Wowo, that's wonderful. My wife will be thrilled. Oh, hey my flight leaves in twenty minutes; I have to call my boy, Ronnie. It's his birthday today. I won't get to see him until tomorrow morning. Okay. All right. Okie dokie, I'll see you at the office then. You better have my plaque ready."

Ricky was always nostalgic for his childhood, even when he was a child. He adored children and making them smile. It just so happened that he, Ricky Malone, stumbled upon a massive market greedy for the simple pleasure of viewing colorful sparkles and patterns through a kaleidoscope. A spark of curiosity and wonder was ignited that would spread across the universe. *This is why I quit selling knives*, he thought to himself.

It would not be long before the entire population of Yurling, Arasthmas, and Konta Banago was completely saturated with kaleidoscope salesmen. Over the next few years, Tyrondu Toys, Inc. became the largest Earthen toy exporter in the universe. The kaleidoscope would then be recognized as the most popular Earth toy ever created. But Ricky Malone would never see the full effect of his labors.

"Ronnie, happy Thursday! Just kidding. Happy birthday, you knucklehead! No, I missed that game. They don't get ESPN 12 where I was staying. I did read that they wanted to get Anderson. But I don't think they have that kind of money to throw around just for a double-dribbling menace."

As the father and son talked about basketball trades, people around Ricky began screaming. Ricky dropped his phone and the last thing Ronald heard from his father was his choking from poisonous gas. As you probably know from the news, a toxic agent had been released into the air ducts, killing thousands of travelers and every working employee in the terminal (this is why rocketports now provide gas masks not just onboard aircraft but also in the lobby).

A memorial service was held; his name read from the pulpit during the service, among the thousands that perished that day. A monument, built across the street from the renovated airport, lists Ricky's name in stone. You are no doubt familiar with the tragic events; the news covered the story for months. They found the perpetrators among the dead, poisoned by their own design. They were members of Humans First, a group opposed to interplanetary travel and cultural exchange, their goal being to shut down all interaction with non-Earth lifeforms, by any means. Years went by since the tragedy. The universe moved on, as it does. Tyrondu Toys moved on. Stella remarried and died at age eighty-five. They buried her next to her first husband.

Ricky Afton Malone
Father - Husband
Kaleidoscope Salesman

The Last Planet

A R Mirabal

We're nearing the end now, or is it the beginning? Floating in the bleak solitude of space we brood, slowly edging further into the fringes of our wit, but unwavering, hopeful.

Our most glaring folly has always been arrogance, but it's also the driving force that's gotten us this far.

Starting as single-celled organisms swimming in primordial goo, we ascended to the height of heights; no nebula too far, no sun unconquered. Our unrelenting will to fight on, to surpass the legacies left by our ancestors, has evolved us past the physical plane into a collective consciousness of energy.

We've weathered countless supernovas, seen what lies through black holes, even mastered the looms of time. We've outlived everything else; we're the last planet.

Just as we've predicted in our infancy, however, the end comes with a whimper, not a bang. The light's dying.

Only a couple stars remain in all the cosmos, and soon those too will die.

Dueling supermassive black holes and lingering asteroids are all that's left in the starless void. The final chapter for life in the universe, after all our strife and resilience, is a long and dry death, but we won't go gently.

Projections of our energy-forms flood the fabrics of space, collecting data and piecing it all together in every conceivable sequence until we crack the last secret this universe holds; there has to be a way to save the light.

Our planet is the last beacon of hope; the final bastion against the darkness.

Warmed by three artificial suns, each siphoning the remaining latent energies that scarcely linger, the planet floats in frigid isolation. Like our physical flesh, the planet's soil is made of nanite-rich organic bionetics: a living, breathing computive intelligence.

Long ago, when the sky still had stars, we infected the infant planet like a plague, hollowed it out and corrupted it, and reformed it in our image.

Now left with the blackness of the void, we defiantly stand in unison to plot our survival. We've exhausted this universe to its limit; we've manipulated the curvature of time, peered into higher dimensions, but still there are no answers in sight.

There is, however, one bell that's yet to be rung. A last ditch effort resulted in the creation of another artificial moon, the largest satellite to date, named Umbra. Its purpose is to simulate endless universes simultaneously.

Broken up into clusters, each cluster is separated by slightly varying parameters; the clusters contain countless universes and each universe is accompanied by infinite alternate copies.

Studying those simulations, we hope to find the missing piece of the puzzle that's eluded our reality. I'm hopeful this will at the very least be an interesting experiment.

v.0.1
Our initial trial failed; the parameters were set too del-
icately, too perfect. It didn't resemble the chaos of our
own universe enough to give us any valuable information.
Improvements will be made for the second iteration.

v.0.2
Our second attempt was a great success, but unforeseen
circumstances corrupted the data. While the program
ran optimally, and was reflective of our own universe, it
appears something in the program became sentient and
started speaking with one of the simulation's operators,
convincing them to spare it from deletion.

The matter's now been resolved; improvements will be
made for the third version.

v.0.3
This will be the last iteration. The experiment, in respect
to our original goal, was a success. Success, however, is
driven by perception.

This third version fixed all the flaws of its prede-
cessors and gave us the data we thought we wanted. What
we didn't foresee was that the same equations we derived
for the salvation of light for a simulated reality, worked
for ours too. It's possible we're in a simulation ourselves.
Obsessively reviewing the data we received, we've been
able to pinpoint structural similarities between space-fab-
ric anomalies and realize that this isn't unique either.

* * *

It seems life truly is resilient to a fault; we've dealt with
this problem in the past, the dying of the light. When
we couldn't find answers before, we projected the last of

our dying essences into a fixed point in the bleak void, a maelstrom of bitter resolve. In it, a fully new universe bloomed, existing (then dying again) in the final breaths of the original universe. Within the copy, scattered remnants of the previous life survived; it was a place for them to reset and experience all of evolution once more.

What's more alarming is that it's impossible to pinpoint the origin. Mathematically speaking, the first universe—a four-dimensional object was copied, creating a three-dimensional "shadow." From the perspective of lesser evolved entities, it's similar to how a two-dimensional shadow is created from light casting onto a three-dimensional object. These shadows, however, aren't few; they're many.

I'm reflective of my original passage in this journal, "Our biggest folly has always been arrogance." It seems that these copies are endless; when the initial copy's time was done, and its light also started to die, another was created in the final moments of the previous. I'm the last of my race; the rest have pooled their energies to create yet another shadow and are projecting themselves into it now.

Watching them in bitter contemplation, light stretches across the black canvas of space as it disappears into a fading dot.

I've decided to inscribe a portion of my energies within this entry and send that into the projection instead. Perhaps it'll be of use there.

I feel the frigid tendrils of the void starting to wrap around me. The artificial suns orbiting us have died a flickering death, and the bitter chill of solitude is beginning to strangle me. Soon, so shall I perish like the stars.

It's been a long time coming, and I refuse to face my end with fear.

Security System Down

Katie Collupy

The wind outside the ground station picked up, shaking
the entire mechanical body as we worked. The ultraviolet
windstorm outside was not unusual for the time of year
on Planet 694, and I calculated that it had only been three
months since the last one had wrecked our station. Once
it passed there would be outside maintenance needed, but
that was work for the outer bots. My work, as it was every
day, would be to ensure that all the locking mechanisms
were secure. The last thing we all needed during a storm
was for more griinae to infiltrate. There were enough of
the ghastly creatures roaming the halls in search of food
despite there being no lifeforms aboard our vessel. There
hadn't been in a long time because the griinae had eaten
the humans into extinction years ago, and there hadn't
been another crew of humans this far out in all that time.
They were the last of them. The griinae simply existed,
becoming bothersome annoyances for the rest of us on the
ship. They roamed and suctioned themselves to the met-

al, rusting the metal underneath them. Griinae multiplied quickly, their blue slime bodies supported by millions of legs underneath, moving quicker than our cleaners. We still hadn't discovered how or when they breed.

Another shake of the station captured my attention, and I returned to my duties. My metal feet carried me down the long dark hallway; the only light came from the fluorescent bulbs and the two giant windows. Along the corridor were cleaning bots, small cubes with large red buttons. They had skinny pinned arms that could elongate to reach the ceiling when they dusted. They were needless little things, and I hated having to interact with them when their batteries ran low. Our solar panel had bent out of shape during the last windstorm, and there were no humans able to fix it.

Loud, steel echoes bounced around the walls as I reached the end of the hall and entered the security room. The overhead lights flickered, and I made a mental note to tell the electric-bots that they needed to be replaced, not that we needed light to see. Our programs would keep us moving until someone rewrote it.

The utter boringness of the routine had started tricking my code into acting out. I attempted to remove myself from my route several times and found myself shutting down. To keep moving I had to keep having the sole intentions of protecting the station.

The station groaned loudly, the start of the shift of the hour. I retreated to the side of the room, bracing myself against the wall, attaching my metal buckle to it as everything shifted. The station had several levels, and as a security measure my programmer had set up a system of clearing that would happen once a day, chemically burning away the griinae or any unfortunate being that didn't find a secure space to hide out.

A midday shift like this one would throw my whole routine off. All of the halls and rooms would change, which meant that there was a chance that someone could sneak into the station unnoticed. That's why I was built. To ensure that the humans would never have to worry about intruders. Once the shift was finished and the station settled again, I unlatched myself from the wall and kept moving. I checked the security room thoroughly. There was not a button or handle out of place.

The sharp sound of something hard hitting the window had me turning back around. I peered at the glass, noticing a long crack running diagonally through the window. I reached out my hand, tracing my metal fingers along it. Something large came flying at me, and I flinched, taking a step back as it shattered the glass. I reached out, opening my arm panel to sound the alarms for the other bots and to make sure a shield would form over the window. The air from the windstorm would rust all of us quickly if it was not contained. We were being infiltrated, but then—

A hand landed on the sill. I paused, staring at it. My mind was working in override, trying to process how someone survived enough in the windstorm to break into the station. The hand was accompanied by an arm, and before I could right myself, a whole body came in through the window. It fell onto the floor, sprawling out and breaking into a coughing fit. I scooted back until I hit the wall. The sound drew its attention my way, and I was met by honey-brown eyes and a sly smile.

"Hello there, bot," it whispered. Its teeth were bright white, and its smooth cream skin was tainted with scars, cuts, and bruises.

I closed the panel on my arm and stood, watching the human closely. *How was it alive? How did it defy the windstorm? Where did they come from?* It rolled over into a crouch, peering at me through a cloaked hood. It brushed away dirty hair from its face and then righted itself, pulling out a clunky metal thing that I searched my inventory for the name of. *It was a knife? No. Gun? No. What was it?* I could feel my wires whirling fast, but I couldn't place the object. I had no word for it in my inventory.

It pulled back its hood, glancing out the window. "Where is your kitchen?"

A long buzz sounded from down the corridor as a red light flashed overhead. "We need to exit the area. This corridor needs to be locked down."

It grunted and then started down the hallway, not heeding any of the caution signs. I watched it go through the metal door, slamming it shut. How curious, it didn't wait for the doors to work automatically. I shook my head and then decided to follow after. It couldn't be left unattended. Hopefully, the other bots would not mind the new presence. There didn't seem to be a choice of whether or not it was going to stay.

I followed through the doors. When I entered the other side, the human's cloak was gone. It was standing over a vent, warming its hands. Its clothes were ragged and muddy, and I assumed it had traveled a long way to get here.

My functions clicked into place finally, and I found my voice, "Do you require service?"

It turned to me, pink circles forming on its cheeks before it chuckled. "Yeah."

I wondered for a moment what she saw when she looked at me, but then my system showed me a picture of myself. I had taken it when I had come across a mirror for the first time. My steel was a dark gray, and my eyes glowed red. I was shocked to find myself looking much like the humans in shape. Most builds were very unique, as the humans never wanted to feel that they were taking advantage of us. If they could separate us and label us machines then we would never be more powerful than them. We would never hold weight in their world.

I forced myself to put away the image and return to the humans service.

"What actions do you wish to be performed?"

"Jeez, they have you hardwired tight," it said.

"Where's your Captain? I need to speak with him immediately."

"Captain?" I questioned. It should know they were gone. "There are no lifeforms present."

"What do you mean?"

"There are no—"

"Yeah, I get that." It moved toward me, and it seemed upset. "What I meant is, what happened to them? Where are they?"

"Krivese attack. The rest were eaten by griinae."

"But the war with the Krivese ended years ago."

"There have been no humans here for three years."

"That's not true," it said, balling its hands into fists. "I got a transmission. A request from this ship to come here."

"Impossible." The communication receivers have been untouched since the humans died. No bot on board knew how to operate them nor were we permitted to do so.

"Shit," it grunted, running its hands through its long hair. "How did… but why…"

"Speak louder."

It whipped its head around, glaring at me. "Be less bossy."

"Your command," I said as I reprogrammed myself.

"Who is in charge then?" it asked.

I took a moment to scan the chain of command order. There were no living lifeforms left, so that left the inventory of bots. Most were tasked with simple chores. "I am."

"Right, and what's your name?"

"Name?"

It sighed. "You don't have one. Of course you don't. The people who lived here are pieces of shit, always have been. So inhumane to their servants."

"I do not understand. You know my masters?" I tilted my head to the side, scanning its face for recognition.

"My friend, he worked on this station. Well, not anymore I guess." It bit its lip before holding out an arm, hand at the end. "I'm Rory."

I placed my hand in its. The warmth from its palm seeped into my metal, heating it. "I have no name."

"Well, are you a boy or a girl?"

I retracted my hand. "I am neither. I am a bot."

"Okay, then let's just call you Cullen," it said. "Now, I'm going to need access to your control room. I have to send a very important message to my station."

"I can take you," I said and motioned toward the door at the opposite end of the room. It was not far, but it would be now unfamiliar to me as the rooms and halls had shifted. I watched it gather its things. It only carried a backpack and its jacket.

Before we left the room, I paused. It looked back at me. "I apologize for being rude," I said. "I should have asked. Are you a boy or a girl?"

It threw its head back and laughed until tears shed from its eyes. "Girl. You're a very strange bot, I hope you know that."

* * *

We finally descended down the new staircase that led to the control room. Rory walked ahead of me, opening up the door and breezing inside. She set down her things on the long table and then retreated toward the control panel. I stood back, against the wall, watching from afar. If she needed assistance she would prompt me.

Her fingers moved carefully across the switches, and then she made a loud groaning sound, turning back around to face me. "How long has it been since you had power in here?"

"The station always has power."

She shook her head. "The panel doesn't work."

I walked over and stared down at the silver panel in front of me. She was right. None of it was lit up like it usually was. *How long had it been since I really looked at it?* I was sure I would have noticed, but it wasn't included in my security protocol, so the chances were that I hadn't. It wasn't my jurisdiction. Besides, who were bots going to contact?

I looked at her.

"Someone's been giving us monthly updates from this panel," she said. "But you said no one has been here for years. I got a message telling me to travel out this way. It doesn't make sense. You aren't even getting power. How could someone send a message?"

"I do not know," I said.

She grimaced, placing a hand on her side. "Okay, we can come back. Do you have any supplies?"

"What do you require?" I said, pulling up my inventory again for whatever she might need.

"Food," she sucked in a sharp breath, pulling up her shirt. A large flesh wound stretched from the middle of her side and disappeared underneath her pants. She looked at me, a frown plastered on her face. "Maybe medicine."

I stepped toward her, and she stepped back. I gestured at her wound. "May I scan it so I can determine the proper treatment?"

She nodded, and I scanned it.

"How did this happen?" It was against system protocol. I did not need the details, but I wanted them.

"Slip and fall." I stared at her, prompting her to go on. Rory sighed. "My rover vehicle broke about halfway through my journey here. I walked the rest of the way, and that windstorm was brutal. I'm surprised I was able to patch up my suit quick enough to avoid the air poisoning." The wound was infected, clearly. It was festering at the sides, a green slime oozing out of it. The bleeding had stopped internally, but she would require her wound to be closed. I knew from my inventory search that we would have the proper materials in any first aid kit onboard.

I stepped back, meeting her level gaze. "We have the supplies you need."

She grunted, pulling her shirt back down. "Lead the way."

I turned from her, stepping back out into the corridor, looking for the right panel to push to deliver an aid kit. All the medical bots had been disabled once the humans expired. I would have to use the kit myself on the human unless she could do it herself.

When the kit arrived, I retrieved a needle and wire. It would not be the most painless procedure, but it was quick.

"I will need to find a table for you to lay upon," I said. Unless the girl laid on the ground, which was mostly sanitary, we would need to move to locate a proper setting.

She pushed herself away from the wall, a clear sheen of sweat across her forehead. She had paled significantly within the moments it took for the bot to bring the kit.

"You are in no condition to move." I lowered myself to the ground, reaching out a hand to pull her down. "We will do this here."

Her cool eyes met mine before she lowered herself. Once she was laying still, I pulled up her shirt and began my work. With every stitch, the girl groaned. Then her sounds of discomfort were replaced by shallow breathing. Once the wound was neatly stitched together, I rubbed a healing salve across the stitches, bandaging it tightly. A quick body scan indicated that she had fainted from the pain, and I scolded my system for not giving her a sedative first.

I had no choice but to carry her to the closest resting area. The human dormitories would be filled with their remains, the bots never daring to go into those shifting corridors that were filled with griinae. Instead, I chose to carry the girl into the bot storage space. It was the place where I remained when I was not on my routine. The metal floor would be uncomfortable, but at least it was clean.

* * *

While I waited for the human to wake, I searched for a shirt and a pair of pants. There was an odd assortment of women's clothing, and I found myself frustrated that I did not scan her for her clothing size. My system was starting to deteriorate against my will, and it was producing active consequences now. I would have to try harder.

I returned to the storage room and set them before her and backed away. "Will these be sufficient?"

She picked at them, pulling out the ones she would change into. "Yeah."

"Then I will take my leave," I stated, turning for the door.

"Wait."

I paused.

"You're just going to leave me here?" she asked. I did not turn around as she changed.

"I have duties that I must attend to," I said. "My programming was interrupted, and I am behind my schedule."

"What kind of bot are you, Cullen?"

Now I turned around. She looked better in the clean clothes, and she had pulled her hair away from her face.

"I need to eat." She walked past me, out the sliding doors and into the hallway beyond.

I followed after her, knowing that we had no food storage. The griinae had eaten through all of our supplies. Did I tell her? I should have, but if I told her then she would leave.

"Cullen?" she asked. "Which way?"

"There is no food." My system heated, and I found myself growing irritated.

She nodded. "Okay, then I need to send a distress signal to my ship."

"You saw the conditions of our control room."

"I did, but I think maybe I can fix it," she said.

* * *

Despite my protest, I sat and watched her work at the control panel. Her nostrils flared and she ran her hands through her hair. Sweat covered her body as she let out another frustrated sound and threw a wrench at the wall. I documented the way she looked when she was angry for future reference.

"Shit," she cursed under her breath. Her eyes scanned the panel. Then a grin broke across her face. "Yes."

Her hands moved across the buttons and keys, turning and pressing options until the screen lit up. She cried out with an emotion I recognized as relief.

I stood to dismiss myself, but when she hit the call button my system stopped me from leaving.

"Alpha System 818, if anybody can hear me this

is Rory Mendeley. I am at location 76539. I repeat, I am stranded at location 76539. Outpost four, I think. Please, if anyone can hear me. I need help. My name is Rory Mendeley. Over."

She stepped back, letting the channel go silent. We waited. The static in the room was deafening. Rory laughed lightly, looking at me. Her face was glowing with hope. The message would be her salvation. I knew from my system that humans could not survive long without food. Especially when they were recovering from a wound.

Minutes passed, and her happiness dwindled.

"Maybe you should try again?" I suggested.

"Yeah, okay." She stepped forward. "Alpha System 818, this is Rory Mendeley. I am stranded at location 76539. If anyone can hear me, please respond. Over."

We waited in the silence again. Rory paced back and forth, rubbing her hands together as she glanced between me and the radio.

My system indicated that it needed a charge soon, but I would not leave Rory here by herself.

Another minute passed. Then ten minutes. Then twenty minutes.

Rory cursed and sat herself down in front of the radio, sending out her message again and again. Nothing came back. Nothing would ever come back.

* * *

For days she repeated her message, her voice growing more hoarse as the hours went on. Each transmission grew more desperate. I left briefly to bring my charging plug into the room so I could stay with Rory. While she sent messages I worked on reprogramming my system so I could remain diverted from my schedule. Over the days,

Rory's wound festered more until she broke into fever. Every hour I brought her water and more blankets, but the fever was taking her body.

I looked over to her curled up body.

"Do you require assistance?" I asked.

Her mouth twitched to a smile. "There's nothing you can do. You're just a security bot. Thanks, though."

"Just a security bot?" I tilted my head. The attempt at a joke to make her smile in this desolate time went against everything my system was taught, but someone had to hold onto the hope.

She frowned. "Don't tell me you're learning emotions now, Cullen."

"Bots can't process emotions," I said, but I knew it wasn't true any longer. Not as the sun set in the sky, and Rory was here alone. Nobody would come for her. But we were at least alone together.

I sat next to her, placing a hand on the porthole. "The outside is beautiful this time of day."

"Have you ever been outside?" she asked, a coughing fit racking her body.

"I've never left the station, no."

"Why not? Your masters are gone. Why stay here?"

I shook my head. "My system wouldn't fare well on the outside. The cold air would deteriorate me quickly as it does all bots. I would be nothing more than rust."

"You can't wear a space suit?" she asked.

It was an idea, but it would probably interfere with my functions too. I remained silent. She leaned over to press the transmission button again for the seventh time this hour.

"Alpha System 818, my name is Rory…" She trailed off, breaking into another coughing fit.

I covered her hand with mine. "Her name is Rory Mendeley. She is stranded at location 76539. If anyone can hear us, please respond. Over."

She smiled at me, but when she opened her mouth only blood came out. Her eyes flashed in fear, and I grabbed her up in my arms. She wiped the blood from her mouth and whimpered in pain. I brushed the hair away from her face, warming my metal for her comfort.

"I'm going to die here, aren't I?" she whispered.

My system rebelled at the thought. There had to be something onboard the ship that could help. Something I could do for her.

"Cullen?"

I looked down at her. "Yes, Rory?"

"Take me outside."

"That's not possible."

"I'm dying, Cullen. Nobody is coming for me." She cupped my face in her hands. "I want to breathe real air one last time."

"Rory, no. It'll suffocate you. Humans were not meant to be—"

"If you don't take me, I'll crawl," she argued.

I nodded, picking her up in my arms and walked her to one of the exit chambers. I stepped inside, closing the inner door after us. I set Rory down, and reached for a space suit, taking one down for her but she shook her head.

"It won't let me feel the air on my skin," she said.

My body rebelled at the idea of taking her to her death, but it was what she wanted. I put the suit back up and opened the outer door.

The chamber let down a cleansing mist as I pressed the button to open the door.

I stepped out onto the sandy terrain of the planet, setting Rory on a rock. The air around started to immediately rust my body. A warning sign flashed over my left eye, and I pushed the panel on the side of my head to turn it off. Rory's breaths grew ragged, and as she choked she grabbed tightly to my hand. I pulled her against me, staring at the sunset before us. The golden light washed over the ground station to our right, illuminating the metal beast in the most beautiful way in contrast to the light blue sand of the planet. Maybe that was how it was always meant to end.

Seven-Year-Glitch

Brenda Radchik

"What's funny, Susy?" Zach asks, a deep frown is drawn on his face. Every day, at some point, he will frown at me.

I anticipate the disgust of his rotten morning breath. But, to my surprise, there's nothing. I give him a small peck on the lips. It startles him. We haven't kissed in over six months. I want to tell him we are funny. And pathetic. *I am laughing at you*. At our charade of a marriage.

We married because our parents told us to. We married because we wanted to have children, even though we were children ourselves. And even *that* hasn't gone as planned.

"Nothing," I say instead, dragging the word as I lean into his chest.

His frown deepens. I crack a smile, wondering if he thinks I'm trying to seduce him. I embrace him and his breath hitches. I inhale and he smells of plastic. Wondering if he is real, I slide a hand under his shirt. His skin is rougher than usual, and his face has a hue of gray. He's usually warm, not this morning though; today his chest feels cold. *Is he ill?*

"What are you doing, love?" His voice wavers.

Now it's my turn to turn still. He never calls me love. I don't like it. Why make an effort now? When we've fallen into the hellish routine we've created since I found him in bed with another person.

Heat fills my face. "Why did you call me that?"

Zach raises an eyebrow as if he doesn't understand, and it infuriates me. I thought we were clear on our silent agreement to stop pretending we love each other. He knows; he must know like I know, that we've hit the seven-year-itch. Just like my friends warned me: *It starts at the anniversary, and then it goes downhill. You'll find him in everyone's bed but yours.*

He keeps staring. I break the pregnant silence. "What happened to you?"

He tilts his head, a gesture I've never seen on him before. I'm sure.

"Whatever do you mean? Come on, let's get up. We have a long day ahead."

It's true. The longest day of the week. Today is Sunday, the reason I didn't hop off the bed; which turned out to be a mistake.

Sundays are for being apart together. For UFO sightseeing in the middle of the desert, where Zach returns with a hundred photographs of sand, while I sleep in the heated car, hoping not to die from the apparent lack of oxygen, since it has no AC.

I think of how he usually smells of bubble gum with a faint layer of Windex and sweat. For some reason, I miss it. "Why don't you smell of anything?" I press.

He sniffs his armpit. "I smell like myself?"

Am I going crazy? I sniff the cheap linen sheets Zach wanted to buy so badly. They smell of me. My eyes turn back to him. He has drifted asleep once more. *Typical.*

When I look at him, I can't help but wonder why we married, and if he feels the same toward me. Once I thought of divorce. Then, I dropped the subject as if it burnt. I will not deal with that until he brings it up. That's what I've decided. Because, I know how it turned out for our neighbor, Maggie. Since her divorce, no one visits. Not even her parents.

I get out of bed, into the shower.

But when I'm drenched in scalding water, I'm drowning in sorrow. It's as if something was snatched from inside me when his smell disappeared. The last connecting bond, leaving behind a void in my stomach.

His smell was awful, yet it was the last thing I could clench to. I don't understand how one can lose one's smell. Just like I can't understand how one can lose a relationship, or memories, or oneself.

It's Sunday, but Zach isn't yelling at me to get ready for *the best day of the week*. I should be happy; this is the first Sunday we haven't gone to the silly sightseeing. I get to spend the day watching TV and drinking beer. We lay on our brown synthetic sofa, and I laugh at the black and white images that project from the TV. Yet, I can't help but feel something is missing.

"Why didn't we go UFO hunting today?"

"UFO hunting? Where?" He sounds baffled.

I stand up, and as I approach him, he makes himself small on the chair. I'm not offended; I already know he doesn't want my touch. I press my hand to his fore-head; it feels inhumanly cold.

"Zach, you're sick—" My words die mid-sentence, the wart on his left cheek is missing. It was there yester-day morning, I'm sure.

"Why don't you lie down, love?"

Love, there's that word again.

He follows me as I exit the room and lie down on our bed. He shoots me a tight smile and closes the door behind him. The TV drowns the sound of his footsteps. I close my eyes but find it impossible to sleep. Thinking of the UFOs usually works, but not this time, not when we've skipped Zach's favorite activity, and he calls me love as if it's nothing.

I open my eyes and stare at the cracked ceiling. I'm sure if we didn't live in such an arid climate, water would've already leaked into our bed.

My mind drifts to the time I was hopeful. Father had come early from work and brought a fountain pen, the first in my collection. Not that I wrote, I just loved the shape and texture, the blot of ink when the silver tip was pushed into paper.

After that, everyone that knew me gifted me a fountain pen on special occasions. So, it didn't came as a surprise when our first anniversary Zach gave me a pen, and the next as well, and the next after that one. A faint smile cracks my frown. I decide to get a look at my col-lection and forget about everything else.

I get out of bed and go into the closet. The pens are always in the safe, next to the dresses. The key is inside my red stiletto. I fish it out and then, slowly; I insert it into the metallic hole. It gives in and I push the door open. Before me is a stack of elegant wood and leather boxes.

A sigh escapes me when I grab the red leather box that contains a purple pen. It's my favorite, a wedding present from Zach.

I briefly glance at the inside and realize that something is different. Zach's things are missing; in their place, there are several folders on the very back of the safe. My hand grazes pen's boxes while reaching for the files. At last, I grab one. It's heavier than I imagined, and a couple of boxes stumble to the floor along with other files and their contents. The ground is upholstered with pages of Zach's life. There are photographs that he told me didn't exist: Zach as a baby, Zach's old house. And there are complicated reports about biology and science, stuff I know nothing about.

When I try to stand, a page crunches under my naked foot, a headshot of Zach, with the mole on his cheek. He lies on an operating table, his guts exposed. I return to the scattered pages below me. When I move them, specks of dust fly, stabbing my nostrils. This provokes a stream of sneezes that can't be turned off. The sneezes stop and my eyes catch a page with my name.
The closet door swings open.

"Zach…" my voice wavers. I remember my mother's advice. *Always act like you're angry, make them think it's their fault, and they'll ask for forgiveness, even if it's yours.* "Zach," I stomp my foot. I don't know how, but this person is not my husband.

"Who are you, really? Where's Zach?" I try to raise my voice, but it comes out as a whisper.

Not-Zach walks past me and grabs a trench coat that's next to the white dress I used on my wedding day.

"You're going out?" I say.

He puts on the trench coat and then buries his hands in his pockets. Then, he raises his left arm, clutching a purple fountain pen, identical to the one in my hand. Before I can ask him why he bought a repeated pen, he points it at my face. He walks two steps and I realize the pen is lined with silver buttons on the edges. He pushes one of them.

When I try to speak, I'm unable to utter a sound; when I try to walk my legs are numb.

"I can't free you until you are trustworthy." He says. "Silence. It is beautiful. Humans talk and talk. Not just the females. All, talk too much."

Not-Zach turns and leaves. I want to lie on the bed; instead, I'm left kneeling for three hours. I am in pain. My legs are cramped and my feet swell two sizes.

He comes back.

"Oh." His eyes widen. "Sorry to leave you like that." He approaches me and I wish I could swallow the lump in my throat. I am draped in his stiff arms. He carries me to the bed and drops me as if I were a carton box. Maybe he'll rip me apart. I imagine my guts hanging at the edge of the operating table like in the pictures of Real-Zach.

He sits on the bed and looks at me. He caresses my ankle.

"You weren't supposed to notice." He takes out the purple pen and does a circular motion in the air. For a moment, my face is free. There's an awful taste in my mouth as if I'd eaten something that burnt.

"I and Zach have been together for seven years. Of course, I'd notice."

"He's observed us for some time, your Zach. We got the signal. We observed back. First as a precaution. Humans are a threat. You hated him."

There's anger inside me, at Zach and his stupidity. At first, I didn't believe there would be such a thing as aliens, but now that I know there is, it seems quite obvious his field trips would make us a target.

"I…" The truth is, I don't know what to say. "We weren't meant to be together but — but hate, gosh, that's a bit much," I say because I'm a hypocrite who can't even admit the truth.

Not-Zach raises his hand to stop me.

"Who are you? A plasticized version of Zach? Is that why you smell like churned plastic?"

He shakes his head, and then his eyes fix on mine. They're empty, it's like looking into the black TV screen. "They think I'm *lost*, Susy. And without them, I might be."

"What do you mean, lost? And who are them?"

He blinks rapidly. "Our planet, Inverprim, is on an expansionist mission. We observed you. The resources on this planet are, as you humans say, top-notch. Observations were made from a distance. And the more I observed, the more I realized… I needed you. And the coordinates, I stole them. They think they were lost in transmission."

I clutch my hands into the crisp sheets, trying to slow my breath. My mind barely processes half of what he said.

"So, when I asked you about going sightseeing, you knew exactly what I was talking about?"

He rubs the back of his neck, in a forced motion. I guess he practiced looking human for some time.

"I didn't want you to find out just yet."

"Why keep the documents in my safe, then?"

He lets out his breath and covers his face with his hands. "I thought it was mostly Zach's. I thought the pens were his."

"Then you didn't observe us enough."

Not-Zach glances in a strange way that reminds me of when Real-Zach attempted to love me. It did little, but he tried.

"They're up there, we're down here." He says, ignoring my question.

"Do you think they'll come?"

A half-smile paints his face. "No. They need the documents."

I don't know what to make of him. There is a part of me that pities him, even though I'm terrified. "I deserve an explanation." Play it brave, that's my card. "What are these documents? Where is Real-Zach?"

He sighs mechanically. "They were going to meet your family. Everything was calculated. There was an agent. She would be you. I," he pointed at himself, "would be him. Together, we would meet the rest of your kind. And then possess each body. They were going to send Inverprim scum to inhabit Earth while extracting precious resources back. There's so much. But they needed the people. Our own bodies would disintegrate from the oxygen excess." He stands. "There are resources such as cobalt. A mineral essential for our machines. And oak to eat. Earth has so much oak."

I want to keep asking questions, my mind is full of them. I ask for the most urgent one.

"Why steal them? The documents, I mean."

He caresses my hand and then looks at his own as if wondering why my touch feels a certain way. "Because we only imprint once. Some people never imprint. I thought that was my case, and then we detected Zach, making his observations and sending ultrasonic waves toward us. Trying to make contact."

I clench my jaw. "Knew it. I knew us coming to those outings…" I grab the sheets and pull them. I don't know what to say. Because it's a lie. I didn't know those outings would result in danger and death. I thought they were a waste of time. That was it.

He stands, and his face is inches away from mine.

"You. Are. My soul. Mate."

He is not. At least not on my part. I thought these things were supposed to be mutual.

"Come." He walks without waiting for me. My legs are cramped but I catch up. He crosses the backdoor, then points his pen at what seems like a random spot in the middle of the backyard. Not-Zach turns the pen and pulls it. The pen stretches an inch, about ten golden miniature buttons are revealed.

His hand trembles, he glances at it and then ignores it. He presses three buttons with his thumb, one at a time.

Not-Zach turns his head and clicks again. This time there are splotches of metal in the air. Like individual pieces of a puzzle. These spots twinkle, until before me is a metallic triangle the size of three cars. I swallow, realizing the structure was here, in our backyard all along. Only it was invisible, and we didn't notice because we never spend time back here anymore.

I suppose it's a UFO, like the one Real-Zach would have killed to have seen.

There's a clicking sound behind me. Before me, a ramp lowers. I get to see a shard of what's inside: blinking red lights.

He walks toward the triangle and stops at the base of the ramp. I try to scream when I realize he's pointing the pen at me.

"Come with me." His voice is raspy, and I wonder if that's what he really sounds like when he's not pretending to be Zach.

I try to shake my head, but my face is frozen.

"If you don't, I will let your body combust in the desert you loved to visit. Or I'll make sure you're blamed for his disappearance."

He releases my face.

"You wouldn't. I'm your imprint."

Lightning interrupts us, white cracks in the sky provide my chance to escape. I run toward him to steal the pen.

He grasps my wrists and clicks his tongue. His reflexes are superior to mine, there's no doubt.

"You're no use to me if you don't come with me and love me."

Without a word, he turns and enters the ship.

I try to run in the opposite direction, but my feet are glued to the ramp. Only when I turn toward the ship I can move. There's one way, and it's forward.

When I climb the ramp the first thing I see is his bareback, silhouetted against the blue lights. I approach him.

"I knew you'd never miss him." He blurts out.

I want to disagree, but it's true, after the loss of his smell there's not much I miss from Real-Zach.

Not-Zach turns and I see his actual face for the first time: it's a formless shadow.

He glances at the button board. I follow his gaze where the fleshy mask of Zach's face is resting above a forgotten mug of coffee, next to the sparkling buttons. He puts it back on and it pops before it merges with the rest of Not-Zach.

"We planned to arrive in seven years' time. In truth, I couldn't wait so long. My lifespan is already halfway wasted."

I take a step back, there is a coldness in the pit of my stomach.

"I'm glad you'll be my partner. We won't have to *empty* you." The way he says it sounds like a threat.

The blinking board is behind me. I try to push a button at random, hoping to activate an escape. He grasps my shoulders and shoves me into the passenger's chair. I bare my teeth at him. "That's not how love works."

"How does love work, *darling*? Don't tell me."

I'm grateful he doesn't want to further the love conversation because he's right. I don't really know how love works. I stare at Not-Zach's dead eyes. I'm afraid to ask, but I have to, one last time because the door is closed and there's no way out. I have nothing left to lose.

"Where's Zach?"

He laughs. "You're looking at him."

"Where's the rest of him?"

He shrugs. "Does it matter?"

"Yes," I lie.

"I consumed his organs to make room for my incorporeal form. Then I plasticized the exterior to prevent the flesh from rot." He pauses, then asks, "Will you be my partner?" He pushes a square button and a drawer below the metallic board opens. Inside is a glided fountain pen, with buttons on the edges, just like his.

And I want to say no. But the pen is beautiful. Besides, there's one thing I want, to survive.

To do so, I have to go with him. In a way, Real-Zach will be alive. His form preserved by Not-Zach, and his soul conserved by me, living his dream. The irony.

"I will," I say and let my hand hover above the glided pen, the first in my new collection.

He nods briefly.

I take it. Electricity runs through my body, first a tingle in my throat, then it lowers until it extends to my feet.

I take his hand and wonder if someday I'll look back and think, *This is love*.

A Gondolier in the Labyrinth

Patrick Moody

In memory of Gene Wolfe

My captain died with her boots on.

Siya, her name was, had a penchant for philosophy when it was just me and her at the till, plying the solar currents between moons. One lesson she repeated often was this: "All you need for a civilization, the only real thing, is a good story. Myths and long memories. That's what it takes."

She gave me a book. Of course, I hardly knew my letters, though I had other things going in my favor. After she placed it into my hand, you can bet I learned my letters. Learned 'em quick. Didn't want to be first mate forever, mind you.

Can't tell you the name of the book. But I can tell you that it was old and made of paper. The kind you see under glass in a fancy museum.

At first, I couldn't make heads or tails of the names, the people, or the places. They confounded me.

Most of the stories were about gods, or what they called gods, and heroes, which were, as far as I could figure, humans like you and me. They were a crude bunch. No strangers to a bit of bloodshed. The heroes weren't all that heroic, and the gods seemed to bicker more than a crew waiting on a long-orbit haul for back wages.

I can tell you, without a doubt, the most important thing I learned from that book is this: human beings, from way back to the days of fig trees and swords and sandals and serpents painted on pots, haven't changed a lick. Not in their souls. Not in their deeds.

Once the mutineers were cleared, and I am not ashamed to admit I took great pleasure in that, we laid Captain Siya in a pod and discharged it from the loading bay. I placed the book in her hands. It was the last thing I did for her.

She wasn't a believer in the Terran god or his ghost son, but I figured the star Hagious would be a good place for eternal orbit. Lots of temples and monkish folk on old Hag's planets. I hope they look up and see Siya floating in their night sky and pray for her. Mithras or the ghost son or the nine-pointed comet that calls men to bleed themselves at dusk… makes no matter. A prayer is a prayer.

Back moonside, I was commended for bravery and offered a captaincy. I declined. Didn't want to haul bio supplies anymore. Didn't have the stomach for it, not without old Siya to whip me into shape and tell me what needed doing. After a time, I accepted a position no sane man would turn down. Turns out Captain Siya had friends in strange places. Strange and high places. Government agents, military brass, real behind the scenes, big-picture movers and shakers, with big desks in shadowy agency buildings.

They asked if I'd ever killed, and I told them yes. They asked if it was justified under Merchant Law, and I said yes; I was pretty sure. That was the size of it. I was to be a captain, all right, but a captain without a crew.

They showed me around the vessel, a gondola, they called it, and I could've sworn the name rang a distant bell. It was a sleek thing, outfitted for pleasure but still offering some firepower.

I stepped aboard and fell in love. She was called the Nine. I asked a woman with a crisp uniform and shiny metals what it meant. She explained that it was a transport ship, built for nine individuals, ten including myself. I'd take these nine to a certain location, drop them off, and wait for one to return. She spoke so quickly and so matter-of-fact I almost missed the last detail.

"One?" I asked. "How 'bout the other eight?"

"You'll be transporting nine soldiers to a testing ground. One will return. For this, you'll receive a captain's salary, full pension, and housing."

"And that… all that, for one trip a year?"

"Correct."

* * *

The moon Luna Minos was lush and green, not too far from the dried, arid husk I'd been raised on. There's a reason I've never been back to Luna Arthuria. The first voyage to the testing ground Labyrinth One was a strange one. I kept my composure for the most part, but being around soldiers makes me a tad bit nervous. Don't know why. Constables, too. I've taken pleasure in fighting, before, but to dedicate oneself to killing for your bread and butter? Something about these folk's state of minds just struck me as odd.

They boarded in silence, six men and three women. I call them men and women, but kids are what they were. Each wore a simple combat suit, lightweight and shining black like insect shells.

I smiled, I think, and welcomed them. Maybe I told them a joke, or said something akin to a joke, just to break the tension. The sprats ignored me completely, their eyes fixed on some distant speck in the horizon. Now that I think on it, them poor kids had a lot on their minds. Some rambling gondolier wasn't worth their time.

Labyrinth One had a single magnetic landing platform, a sleek metallic disc set into the cliff face. Aside from attaching and detaching, I had nothing to do but wait. I wished them well. Can't remember the exact words. I'm sure I stumbled over them, and I'm sure none of them heard me, anyhow.

They rose; all tensed up, I could even tell beneath the combat duds. They unloaded their packs. Knives. Rope. Guns. Swords. Lights. Typical gear. They armed themselves on the platform. Silent as gravetenders.

That was the damndest thing. Weren't soldiers supposed to be the most talkative before a fight? That's when all that bonding happened. Battlefield camaraderie.

The nine soldiers marched single file into the mouth of the Labyrinth. I thought of them thick-headed heroes from the paper book, naked men and women in nothing but leather sandals with magic swords the crazy godlings gave them. The heroes messed around in caves with fire in their blood and blood on their steel.

I hoped them kids were smarter than those heroes.

I waited most of the afternoon until the blue moon rose and the sky turned that sleepy shade of purple. Footsteps woke me from a daydream. Loud, harsh things, banging and clanging in the dark, until one of the soldiers, I think it was one of the soldiers, stumbled out onto the platform.

Her skin wasn't skin anymore. I know that's a terribly unhelpful way of putting it, but it's the honest truth. She limped into the ship with feet no longer feet, and gripped the seat with hands that weren't quite hands. Mostly, it was her eyes that struck me. Glass, I think, or some kind of plastic.

"You… you alright, private?"

Her face changed. Colors shimmered. Her voice sounded like something you'd get over a bad comm link, like the disturbance when there's too much radiation in the atmosphere, you know?

"I am Onda, the champion." It was a fuzzy, metallic croak. "I am ready for deployment, gondolier."

An arm that wasn't an arm bent up in a confounding angle.

Too many joints.

I returned the gesture with a weak salute. My guts burned something fierce.

* * *

I was twenty when Captain Siya's corpse joined the stars. It's been forty years since I took this job. My hair is white. My teeth are all new. My bones creak, and my back aches something terrible when the white moon makes its wintry visit. But I can still mend sails, and work the till, and navigate the stars.

The survivors scared me to death, each one of them. I asked the woman in brass where the survivors ended up.

"They serve on the holdout moons," she said. "Tip of the spear."

"Super soldiers?" I'd heard of such things.

"No," she said. "Heroes."

That was all I could get out of her.

Forty heroes.

Three hundred and sixty dead children playing at war.

It had become routine. Natural as spit. The would-be heroes boarded the Nine, and I flew them to Labyrinth One. I've aged. The heroes never do.

We landed on the strip. It was cold that morning, and my knee was acting up fierce. I settled in for a long, painful wait, dreaming of a hot shower back home.

The kids got ready on the platform. Belts with blades and firearms. One had a spear. Another sharpened some kind of ax whose head looked like blue-tinted glass. Three had new fangled weapons, something to do with sound waves. Big suckers they slung over their shoulders, barrels the size of a grown man's arm. They looked silly, really, but I knew better than to scoff at military tech.

As they marched, the boy bringing up the rear stumbled. A knife slipped from his belt. The wind was howling so loud at the cave mouth I don't think he even heard it drop.

"Hey!" I yelled over the wind. "Hey! Private! You dropped—"

He disappeared, swallowed by the cave mouth.

The knife skidded across the platform. I hopped off to pick it up. The thing was huge. Serrated, like the kind hunters have on the green moons. The kid's name was etched on the wooden hilt.

Parker, Kenji

"Oh, hell," I muttered. Thing must have been at the kid's side his whole time though bootcamp. It was old and worn, and had to have been a family heirloom.

I'd never been inside Labyrinth One. I had orders to stay out, for one. Second, the champions scared me so bad I'd started taking pills for the nightmares.

I hefted the blade, feeling the wood grain against my palm. Hadn't gripped a knife that big since I'd dispatched the last of the mutineers all them years ago. Heirloom or not, I had no business holding it.

But Kenji did.

Hell, he'd probably be needing it soon.

In a moment of absent-mindedness, the heirloom knife dropped point first through my boot. I let out a pained hiss, afraid to even look. But I had to. With a grunt, I extracted the knife from my foot. There was a first aid kit on the gondola, but that would have to wait. Blood pooled from the soles of my boot around me like a maroon lake.

* * *

Labyrinth One was quiet. Dark as sin, too. I reached down to my belt, blindly exploring with shaky hands until I brushed my flashlight. A welcome orb of clean, white light enveloped me like an egg. The walls weren't stone like I figured they'd be, it being built into the side of a cliff and all, but smooth alloy carved here and there with runes. Military runes, I realized, and took a step, stubbing my toe on a rock. I lowered the light and found the floor littered with them. It was rough going, and I had to lift my knees high every aching step, like hiking through woods when roots twist up like petrified snakes waiting for an ankle to break.

A scream bounced off the walls and set my molars vibrating. Labyrinth One seemed to be nothing but hallways, and none of them were straight. They branched off and wound, sometimes bending in sharp turns. They forked, and some just ended with a flat wall. The runes started making me dizzy. I tried not to look. Bloody things, they were. Obscene.

A few pistol shots rang out, and when they did I crouched down, thinking of the ricochet, as I couldn't tell where the damned things were coming from.

Further on, down where the runes grew more numerous, the walls of Labyrinth One were coated in dried blood. It looked like rust, only I smelled it, all coppery and stringent, and soon came upon some that wasn't so dry. Puddles of it. Smears. Drops. Rivulets trickling around old yellowing bones.

I stopped at a fork. One of the kids was on the floor at the head of the left path. He was dead. I don't know where his lower half was. With my torch in one hand and Kenji Parker's knife in the other, I stepped over him.

Never noticed just how white the spine is.

Wasn't long before I found the soldier's lower half. It was slumped against the wall, like he'd been sitting there catching a breather. Another turn, and I found one of the girls. She'd been impaled right through the wall. Luckily, and I say that for my own sake, she'd been pinned face-first. I don't think I'd have had the stomach to look her in the eyes.

The maze stretched on through dark serpentine curves. Craggy, uneven floors and unusual acoustics made me think perhaps I was suffering ear damage from those new sound weapons. My knees were screaming. My foot was bleeding. The handle of Kenji Parker's knife was slick with sweat. But I kept on and passed more of the kids. None of the bodies were Kenji Parker.

Some were fresh, but most were skeletons, or close to it. I recognized some of the faces, whose flesh hadn't sloughed off.

A roar brought me to my knees, and with it came a smell, like an electrical fire. My nose ain't what it used to be, takes something real powerful to catch my notice.

The hall broadened, ending in a circular chamber. The runes were big, telling their crude and nightmarish tales.

The roar was close now. I clicked off my flashlight and crouched in the shadows. Didn't do any good. With a loud pop, greenish light from long bulbs flooded the corridor.

Kenji Parker and the last cadet were there. They huddled in the center of the room, whispering. I thought about calling out to them but stopped myself.

Something else was in there with us.

It was big, moving in thunderous clops through the thick bundles of smoking wire that hung down like vines. Large glass tubes lay cracked and strewn on the floor. In the center was one of those nuclear batteries, the kind that keep the colder moons heated and lit.

It powered a great mess of a machine. Gears and mechanical arms, pincer-like things, saws and tubes of fluid. A dented table was set in front of it. The sound it made was deafening. I recognized it as an automated surgery unit, or ASU for short. It rumbled and shook, ear-piercing beeps and bangs, sputtering now and then with deafening blasts like a backfiring ship's engine.

Sinister, but the strange operating station wasn't what kept me crouched in the darkness. It was the thing in there with us: tall, stalking through the wires. It roared again, the power behind it strong enough to overtake the ASU, and when it did, I heard something like the hissing of a hydraulic pump. A large hand, maybe a paw, swiped a mess of cables out of the way, allowing its full form to step out into the clearing.

Steam poured out of what I took for its mouth.

The last cadet charged with her spear, the tip ablaze with blue flame. The thing, machine, I realized, swatted the weapon away.

The mechanical creature stood twice her height, composed of a matted metal. In a blinding motion, she drew her pistol and thrust the muzzle under its jaw. She managed three rounds before it took her leg with one hand and her arm with another and lifted her over its head. Metal joints creaked, more steam issued from its bull-like nostrils. With a grunt, it yanked her down upon its two horns with such force that she was immediately impaled, one through her neck, the other through her liver. She didn't cry out. Didn't have time.

Another mechanical hiss, another roar, and the beast was upon Kenji Parker. I cried out to him before the hulk struck, and even aimed to toss him the knife. My voice was strained in my throat. Instead of fighting back, Kenji Parker let his arms drop to his sides, his weapons forgotten, and saluted the machine.

The monster regarded Kenji, the cadet's gore still dripping from its horns. I'll be damned if the thing didn't kneel before that boy, prostrating itself like the rookie soldier was some kind of divine being.

The creature lifted Kenji Parker and placed him on the ASU.

What followed was butchery. Plain and simple. Quick, precise butchery, and when it was done flaying the skin and peeling back muscle, sawing bones and inserting wire and metal rods, the boy wasn't a boy anymore.

I just watched and waited until the heap on the table drew in one big, heaving breath, though it couldn't have been breath, more like that hiss the horned one made.

The new soldier stepped off the table, unsteady on its new bearings, so I rushed to help.

"You were to wait at the ship," he said. The eyes were so round and glassy that there were no pupils, so I couldn't tell if he was really looking at me.

I held out the knife, hilt first. "I thought you might need this."

His head jerked down. "No."

"I saw you drop it on your way in."

He didn't answer. I didn't expect him to.

"You know how to get out?"

It stooped down until its reflective face was level with mine. "We must find it ourselves."

"How are we going to do that?"

He pointed to my bleeding foot. "Your bio stream will lead us from this place."

Once aboard, I dialed up the engine as it blinked to life.

We flew in silence. He didn't look at me. I don't know if he ever truly had.

I offered the knife for the last time.

"I have no need for it."

I slipped the blade into my good boot. Thought about shipping it back to the Parkers, whatever moon they called home. In the end, I kept it. It has served me well ever since.

I brought us up atmosphere side, studying the smattering of stars. It took a while to spot Hagious, and I wondered if Captain Siya circled it still. I wondered, too, if the paper book was still intact inside the glass coffin. Myths and long memories, she'd said. That's all it took. Damned if she was right.

A Fistful of Credits

Alex Child

The slavers were on edge. Every clatter within the Demeter's dilapidated heating system was met with an unholstered antimatter pistol and a series of expletives strung together with a finesse unique to spacers. Tension spread through the ship's hallways like cosmic radiation despite the lockdown. It was always like this while docked at remote ports of call to deliver its cargo of ingestible euphoria, the hallucinogenic drug millanora.

Even on Callisto, the largest of Jupiter's moons and farthest humanity had expanded thus far; interplanetary peace officers made a habit of inspecting docking stations. Getting caught with drugs was bad, but getting caught with slaves was even worse. The crimes of kidnapping and forced labor had been recently upgraded to A1 felonies. A conviction came with a lifetime sentence of hard labor on a lunar mining colony.

Two enslaved bunkmates, Huxley and Briggs, stared at the frayed metal panels of the ceiling. There was little else to do until the clock buzzed, indicating their next meal, if a spoonful of preserved oats, protein substitute, and a glass of water could be considered a meal.

Time passed mysteriously beneath the constant fluorescent bombardment. Minutes passed quickly when one was violently dragged across the floor. However, months bled into one another, forming a stretch of time that Huxley could no longer quantify.

Huxley's eyelids sagged, relenting to the fatigue of knowing every corner and crack and line of his surroundings. But he fought sleep. He hated dreaming. Huxley hated a lot of things. His captors. The ship. And even though there was no reason for it, he often hated Briggs. But in this moment, it was his hatred of dreaming that bubbled to the surface, forcing him to rise from his bed and stretch his legs.

It didn't matter if he napped for five minutes or eight hours, he always dreamed. He used to envision his loved ones at home, celebrating a holiday, or gathered around the table for a meal. But something in his mind had changed. Now, his mind only re-ran surreal copies of an average day aboard the ship: plucking, drying, and distilling millanora leaves. It was as if the mental tapes of his pleasant memories had crumbled to pieces and now were lost.

The feeding bell sounded, and two servings of powdered sustenance spilled from a metal chute into a single bowl as their water tin filled three-quarters full. Huxley was grateful that his bunkmate split the food evenly. His last bunkmate licked the bowl dry if he got to the food first.

They had just finished eating in silence when the grated door opened and Cato, one of the supervisors, stomped inside, "Sewage pipe burst. Both of you, out."

The two snapped to their feet. Cato led them down the grease-stained hallway. Pipes leading in every direction hissed and sputtered beneath flickering lights.

Cato handed them two scrub brushes and a bucket of soapy water, then sealed them in the lavatory. Huxley worked with vigor, having discovered early in his servitude that physical exhaustion helped dull the senses. He got to work mopping up a sewage puddle while Briggs rummaged through their tools in search of tape. Their faint shadows copied their repetitive movements as the sound of Cato's footsteps faded.

Briggs pressed an ear to the locked door.

"Think we're good," he said with a raised thumb.

Huxley stuck a finger through a hole in one of the floor tiles, and pulled a small transmission receiver from the dusty crevice. It was old and covered in filth, but thanks to Briggs' handiwork, still functional. At least in short range.

Briggs toyed with the dials, manipulating them until the diode turned green. A staccato voice, its pronunciation firm and deliberate whispered through the bathroom:

> *... the genocidal warlord was later released after the interplanetary courts ruled the evidence in his conviction was obtained illegally. His current whereabouts are unknown, and charges against the peace officers involved are expected in the coming days.*

The news was always bleak, but they didn't listen to escape their present circumstances. They listened to remind themselves that there was a world beyond the hulls of the Demeter, where ordinary people were free to live their mundane lives.

> *... Earlier today, legislation was approved by the Interplanetary Ministry of Justice, granting clemency to any enslaved participants in the galaxy's ongoing war with euphoric hallucinogens. Any and all forced laborers will be granted asylum and receive government-funded assistance...*

Huxley paused, "Did… did you hear that?"

Briggs smiled, "Sure did. It's about goddamn time."

The two paused, as if any additional movement would somehow hamper the soundwaves coming from the makeshift speaker.

… In an attempt to encourage the public to come forward with information leading to the arrest of deep-space slavers, there will be hefty rewards of up to two million credits for any information leading to the arrest of slave traffickers.

"Did you hear that? If we find a peace officer, we're free and clear!" said Briggs.

"Do you know what I could do with two million credits?" Huxley said.

"Hey, you know what it says, 'lay not up for yourself treasure on earth, which corrupts.'"

"Good thing we're not on earth!" Huxley said, then with a smile, he added, "I have an idea."

The cleanliness of the bathroom suddenly seemed unimportant. Between hushed discussions, the pair made plans.

* * *

Another hour passed before Cato returned. His whistling resonated down the hallway and bounced off the rusted walls.

Once the door opened, Huxley hit Cato over the head with a metal broom just as Briggs splashed a bucketful of cleaning solution into his face. Adrenaline lit a fire in the two captives, adding a level of strength to their actions that would have been unthinkable even a few hours earlier.

Cato screamed, eyes clenched shut. One hand wiped his face while the other frantically reached for his pistol. But Huxley and Briggs were too fast. Huxley lifted the clasp of the holster, leaving Briggs free to pull the gun. Then in a single, fluid motion, Briggs fired a shot through Cato's temple. Cato fell like a sack of condensed millanora seeds.

They stripped the officer, and Huxley handed the outfit to Briggs and said, "You're better with a weapon."

"Comes with the training," Briggs said as he put on the outfit. He checked the supervisor's pockets. He felt a wad of cash and an even bigger wad of millanora that he kept to himself.

They carefully walked out into the hall, empty apart from them, then locked the bathroom behind them.

Huxley crouched, half-running behind his armed companion. Briggs carefully swept each corner with the pistol clenched in both hands. Huxly kept a sharp eye on the doorways and entrances behind them, just as they had planned.

To the uninitiated, the labyrinthian hallways blended together in an intangible sea of dull metal and clanking pipes, but years of enslavement had imprinted each imperfection into the captive's mind.

They ran through the galley, passing a pair of crewmen eating meat and potatoes with gravy. Real meat and real potatoes, instead of rehydrated meal packets in a filthy bowl. As Huxley's stomach churned with desire, one of the crewmen looked up from his meal and recognized him.

Without hesitation, Briggs shot two of the men dead, and with even less hesitation, Huxley shoved two meaty handfuls of food into his mouth as a crewwoman on the other side of the galley triggered the alarm. Briggs shot her in the back.

The alarm wailed from the ship's intercom system. Shouting from distant rooms amplified, then came shots firing passed them, but neither fugitive noticed as they broke into a sprint when the Demeter's docking ramp came into view.

The pistons surrounding the door hissed and clattered to life as a shot struck the wall just over Huxley's head. Briggs fired back, but Huxley didn't dare turn around. He pressed his shoulder against the door, not caring that it would do little to expedite the door's opening.

After several painfully-long seconds, the door finally creaked open, releasing a rush of artificially filtered air and sending a tremor of hope through Huxley's spine.

A few haphazard bursts of antimatter fire peppered the walls as the pair dashed into a slim, bare hallway. It wasn't until they sealed the door that a wave of crushing relief expunged the air from Huxley's lungs.

They stood on a platform leading to a busy thoroughfare bustling with commercial activity. They immediately entered a throng of shoppers, disappearing quickly into a sea of pumping legs and bumping shoulders.

A few bystanders peered at them, but none stared too long.

They walked through the marketplace of new gizmos. Huxley was memorized by the four dimension television set, with accompanying the psychic surround sound. *You could buy anything with credits.* His mind raced over the lost years he'd spent toiling away; willing to trade anything to get it back.

"Halt, citizens!" a uniformed officer approached Briggs. "Hands in the air!"

A second officer came up and said, "I'm Officer Kowalasky and this is Officer Grendall. We detected a trace of Millanora on your person."

"We were just on a drug ship called the *Demeter*—" Briggs explained.

"I was a slave, and I escaped! And this guy," he pointed a finger at Briggs, "pursued me! If you don't arrest him, he's going to take me back!"

"Do you have drugs on you, sir?" Kowalasky asked.

"No drugs, just this gift." Briggs pulled out the drug and handed it to the first officer.

Kowalasky smelled it, then raised his brow. "This is pure shit."

Grendall leaned over, covering a finger in the package's contents and licking it. "Woo! I'm gonna see ghosts tonight!"

Dumbfounded, Huxley snapped, "What are you doing? You should be arresting him! He *enslaved* me. I want my reward."

Kowalasky said, "We have to follow procedure before we make any arrests."

"Yeah, you've got to fill out a Q96 form before accusing anyone of felony enslavement," Briggs continued, winking at Huxley.

"Oh, this guy really knows his peace-keeping procedure." Grendall said, nodding.

"I used to serve on the 877 Precinct," Briggs said.

"Oh, no way! My uncle was the retired captain."

"Captain Addleburg?"

"Yes!"

"Wow! Tell the old bastard Briggs said to, 'watch out for falling bricks!'"

Grendall laughed, slapping Briggs on the back. "Oh, man, you're a riot!"

Huxley glanced at his feet, wishing he'd had the money to purchase an invisibility emitter.

Kowalasky interjected, "Well, we still have this serious felony here."

Briggs pulled out a wad of at 10,000 credits. They crinkled in his hand. "Will this cover it?"

Kowalasky pocketed it without counting. He nodded. "Thank you for the donation to the peace officers' retirement fund."

Huxley looked between the officers, then shoved Briggs. He started to run, but Kowalasky grabbed him and pinned him down.

"I am a teacher from Ohio. I was kidnapped while on a field trip over a dozen years ago!" Huxley cried.

"Muzzle this guy so I can send a clear transmission," Kowalasky said as Grendall tightened a muzzle over Huxley's mouth. "Dispatch, this is Unit 612. False alarm. We're escorting the suspects back to their ship."

Briggs clicked his heels together and offered an exaggerated salute, "Protect and serve, commander."

Halloran's Truth

Virginia Babcock

"All the histories indicate the Halloran disappeared on that ship. If this is not him, then where is he?" Putter says to Victor, his mission supervisor and friend.

Victor's growing frustration is clear in his tone. He continues, "That can't be the Halloran! No females were allowed to lead us before Terra fell."

Putter replies, "This has to be him, uh, her. All the identification codes match the Halloran, even if all the data indicate his gender was male. Couldn't she have been the first director? Most of our directors have been female. Statistically, they are better suited to the job." He pauses, standing in the middle of sickbay, "Of course, our current director is male…"

"Stay focused, Putter. We need more data." Victor pulls him forward. "He can't be a she. Instead of a priceless find, they'll think this ship's a fraud. They laud his monkish lifestyle and driven focus for the Consortium succeeding. A female would have been laughed out of the galaxy."

"We both know 'story' starts from truth, but it can lose its veracity over the centuries." Putter stares at Victor. With the Thirteen Families scheming to take control from the Consortium, the University desperately needs to find the Founder. The payoff from the information would fund the planet's needs for decades. More than that, an identity was paramount to the Consortium because if the wrong group found the Founder, they could claim him as their own and reignite a war likely to cause the Consortium to fall.

For years Victor and Putter had searched for the lost flagship, Algol of the Consortium's first armada. After centuries of treasurer hunters searching and scientific expeditions, they had finally discovered the Algol orbiting an uncharted planet only identified through a single mention in the archives. The lost ship was a treasure of ancient technology and included the First Director's original library. Finding the possible corporeal remains of their founder is a wonderful and barely-hoped-for surprise.

Victor scrutinizes the ancient and rare body preservation pod. "Can you imagine if Director Unity was here? He'd order us to place this pod in Consortium's central hall where the statues of the Thirteen families' first borns could stare down on it, knowing they've finally been usurped."

Putter's tone betrays his worry, "I hope the life preserving functions didn't fail."

Victor speaks, "We've opened pods from the First Insurrection and revived those members. A thousand years of improvements should have protected the Halloran."

"Of course!" Relieved, Putter pats the heavy medical corpus retriever floating in front of him. Another thought hits him: "The Halloran was unfailingly generous. Maybe he saved this woman for some reason?"

Neither can add more voice to the fear they share. If it's not the Halloran, war will be inevitable.

Victor shakes his head. "Raising the lid." He applies the antique tool they'd found in the ancient ship's sickbay to the multi-level locking mechanism above the unknown female's head. "Either way, we'll know her true identity shortly."

Both men step back and hold their breath out of habit as the transparent lid slides open, revealing a female body coated in a protective clear blue coating. Their helmets protect them from vacuum in space and airborne toxins in the atmosphere like the stale air on the Founder's ship, but not smells; especially noxious odors that could remain in a suit's air tubes until flushed. Instead of putrid rotting flesh, their air cyclers pull in the clean scent of citrus and flowers.

The men study the specimen. Her pale face has dark lashes and a bruised cheek. A first generation Consortium space jumpsuit garbs the figure from neck to fingers and toes.

"She's flawless," Victor says.

Putter remarks, "She's dressed for the era and has the Founder's dark hair. Could the Founder have been gender dysmorphic?" Though doubtful, Putter tries to placate him. "You know it's possible. Maybe this is his companion?"

"No way. The Halloran was celibate. No female was worthy of him."

Putter says, "Remember those rumors that his genetics were defective and should be kept from our lineage?"

"Again, the genetic arguments at the time hinted at imperfections, giving no specifics. I don't observe any in this body. Besides, that tripe was only documented in the second century and was discounted years ago. The Halloran was healthy, but he had too many admirers. He remained isolated to avoid infighting."

The medical cart locks the body pan into its new cradle. The arm retracts into the cart's base, and the cover closes. A glowing light heralds the start of the thawing process.

Putter grabs the tow bar and turns the loaded and humming medical cart toward their ship. Victor walks in pace with him as they cross the width of the derelict.

At the airlock, Victor speaks, "Lock release." The heavy apertures from both ships spin open from the center, revealing the airlock. Its stiff, articulated segments connect their ship to the Founder's. Victor leads them at the foot of the cart. Putter takes position behind, looking down at the female's face. The airlock is just big enough to hold them and the cart.

They stand patiently as the decontamination spray spritzes them. Years of experience have taught both that nothing can hurry a proper sanitation, giving them time to think. The floor glows as it heats the soles of their space-suits to neutralize chemicals and microbes. Though their face screens protect them, both instinctively blink eyes as the solar lights dry the micro spray. A new smell of Terran-mint fills their helmets as the final purification step sterilizes their airways and lungs.

A rumbling vibration accompanies the inner door opening. Once it closes behind them, Victor de-suits first. Putter pauses a moment before stripping from his space-suit and trailing him to their sickbay.

Putter addresses the medical computer, "Dock medical cart. Order cellular identification." The medicart moves forward to the far wall. Its resting dock rises from the floor and engages the magnetic couplers with a series of loud clicks.

Despite the Founder's DNA being classified, the Consortium authorized a partial DNA sequence for their research. As the body thaws they begin the arduous process of collecting and cataloging samples for tissue and organ preservation before repair.

* * *

Two days later, early in the morning, Victor wakes in his bunk from a dream of the gorgeous unidentified woman and races to sickbay to view her. Her clothing has been removed and sterilized. The 48-hour rejuvenation process was nearly complete.

The final medical report is ready. It gives one expected diagnosis and another unexpected fact. The female died as a result of a viral infection, but is otherwise healthy. Incredibly, the body showed signs of many childbirths, including one that must have occurred only days prior to death. Females had ceased to serve as birthing vessels years before Terra was destroyed. No one in the days of the Halloran or since has been born outside of a medi-tube.

The machine beeps, and the woman's eyes open. She looks around and smiles at Victor.

* * *

An incoming message wakes Putter in his quarters. Worried the Consortium could alter the DNA results to protect their rule, Putter had asked a colleague working in their lab to independently confirm the true results. Like he and Victor, this contact risked her life if the Consortium or the Thirteen Families identified her as a mole. The encoded message from his contact is garbled. Eventually he reads,

> "SECURE:::Gen results confirm corpus = Hall.
> Corpus = mother of all first children. 'Ware
> Con. Will falsify report. Stay far. Prax. only
> 'fuge.:::SECURE."

It's true then. The Halloran was… is female. And the Consortium will lie. This news can only lead to chaos. Putter shudders, overcome as the reality of their situation settles in.

He sends a message to Victor about the results, but he doesn't answer.

Putter queues the ship's internal video feed and searches for his colleague. He curses the two-minute archiving delay. Finally, he locates Victor in the resurrected arms of the Founder as they lie together in the medi-cot. Putter sprints to sickbay and trips and falls over Victor's collapsed body. A pair of bare feet step up to Putter. He looks up at the Founder's naked form. She bends, and a sharp pain blossoms in his neck.

She pulls a syringe from below his jaw and grabs for his genitals. He hears her words as he fades to unconsciousness, "I require your genetic material."

* * *

Victor shakes Putter awake. Putter blinks and tries to sit up. They are in the Founder's ship, sprawled in the hallway next to the control room.

Victor snaps, "Come on! We need to see if this thing can run. The fuel cells are full, but she's already headed to Capsa on our ship." Victor is wild-eyed, pressing buttons on the closest wall terminal frantically. "The fuel cells are full. We could maybe catch her."

"No! We need to go to Praxaton. The Founder is the Mother of the clans. It's our refuge." Putter closes his eyes as he tries to think.

"The Mother?" Victor asks.

"Remember how the original thirteen captains in Halloran's unit returned from war with their wives and firstborns to settle Capsa? Those wives weren't the mothers of those children, they, the originators of the Thirteen Families, were born of the Halloran, the Founder. She copulated with all her captains."

"She and I…" Victor trails off.

"Yeah, I saw you in the cart with her. Putter clears his throat. "Did she… use me, too?"

"Yes. But don't worry about that now," Victor pulls on Putter's arm, "try to stand. I don't know what she hit us with, but the drug seems to wear off the more you move. Your limbs may be asleep. My suit's internal clock shows most of the day has passed."

Both are unsteady on their feet, boots clanking against the floor with each step, but they finally reach the control room.

Victor looks at the main control panel and sits in one of two nearby seats. "Damn, she must have programmed our departure for us. We don't have time for me to change it." He scrutinizes the screen before stating clearly, "University coordinates confirmed."

Putter shakes his head, feeling the effects of the drug finally leave his system, then he sits himself in the seat beside Victor. Flexible, security straps drop from the ceiling directly overhead. Both men click the ends of the straps to connectors on their suits. Out of habit, they check the locks on their helmets at the neck joint, verifying internal life support is ready.

Their seats collapse into the floor as the gravity shuts off and they float up, halting in the center of the room. They wait, secured in place at the limit of the straps. The huge viewscreen lights up to show a forward view of the space outside. The ship moves out of orbit. The planet gets visibly smaller as they pick up speed.

Victor speaks first, "We'll find her."

"How can you be so confident?"

"Because these holding straps have clasps that work with our suits. The Halloran left us in her ship, knowing that we'd survive the journey. She wants us to follow her."

"Why?"

"She needs disciples. She wants us to spread the word about her return. The more people know about her, the stronger she gets, and the easier it is to create a new dynasty."

"And a war?"

"To determine who will govern us once and for all."

Beware Of Beings In The Sky!

Dylan Colón

(Present Day)

Brandon used to warn me about the beings in the sky.

They became an obsession of his, consuming his thoughts and time. Tonight, I find myself on my back porch, looking at the stars, and missing the way things used to be. We used to do normal things like hang out with our friends and drink at the bar, but that had been three years ago. Before the beings in the sky.

This has been a long recovery for my mental health. Mostly because people don't believe me when I try to explain what happened the last night I saw Brandon. It's been a while since I've talked to anyone about it. My therapist thinks it's time for me to try again, engage my trauma, and put the broken pieces back together. He suggested I spend some time alone to revisit those difficult memories. So, now I'm inhaling a cigarette in the cold, blowing smoke into the starry sky, as I try my best to recall the events of that terrible night.

(3 Years Ago)

I showed up at Brandon's house. He had carved out a little space for himself in his parents' home, a tiny dark room with his only window boarded up. Scattered across the floor were molded food and empty liquor bottles, and dirty clothes lay in discarded piles.

At this point in our friendship, we didn't watch movies anymore. Brandon wholeheartedly believed the beings in the sky communicated with him through the character's dialogue. We also didn't listen to music anymore because he feared what they would say to him through the lyrics. Over the passing weeks, his eyes had grown wider, their redness resembling the veins in my wrists, all restless and strained.

Brandon worried about me all the time. What I was watching, what I was listening to, where I was going, and who I was becoming. He was convinced the beings in the sky would take me as they took him on two different occasions. This was always a difficult conversation because I could see his frustration. Even when I wasn't bluntly disagreeing, listening just wasn't enough for him. He knew I didn't believe.

If I'm being completely honest, this was a moment in time where I would have given anything to believe my brother-in-arms. Because at least then, he wouldn't have felt so misunderstood and delusional. How could I communicate? If I mentioned a celebrity, I was accused of being brainwashed by the beings who wore their skin. If I mentioned a song, he would tell me their sonic mind control manipulated me. If I brought up a movie, then my mind was stained by the illusion they shot through my eyes. If I simply just listened… it just wasn't enough support.

What's worse? Knowing Brandon lived in a nightmare? Or living in a nightmare caused by Brandon?

One night, I slept at his house, and he violently shook me awake.

"Wake up, Tyler!" he whispered frantically, shaking me until I responded.

"What is it?" I said, yawning.

"Come outside, Tyler! It's them! They're in the sky, and they're talking to me!" he yelled. His eyes were bloodshot and restless. I was thinking about how I gotta get the hell out of here, but instead, I followed him through the dark hallway and to the back door. His parents had built this beautiful porch that overlooked the backyard like the Milky Way overlooking eternity.

I shivered with my arms tucked tightly against my body. "What's going on?" I asked. My breath was a misty haze with every word I spoke.

"You see that, buddy?" said Brandon, pointing at the night sky.

I stood there in the cold and searched intently for anything that didn't look like the millions of stars that sprinkled the heavens.

"I don't see anything, bro. I just see the stars. What am I looking at?"

He scoffed, his face crimson. "Up there, dude! Look! They're talking to me!"

I looked harder even though I knew he wasn't seeing anything. It was colder than my ex-girlfriend outside, and I just wanted to go home. I squinted harder and saw blinking lights past the dark clouds, but it was a satellite.

"It's a satellite, Brandon."

"I'm not talking about that! Look! Right there, Tyler!" He jerked his finger in the direction of an airplane with blinking lights.

"That's an airplane."

"I know that's an airplane! I'm not talking about that! Why can't you see it? It's literally right there in our faces! Look at the signal lights!"

"Dude… I see them…" I lied.

Was I a bad person to lie? I was scared of Brandon because I didn't know what he was capable of. The doctors said he had schizophrenia. My mom grew up knowing a kind lady that was killed by her schizophrenic son.

He danced in excitement. "I told you they were real! I told you they came to see me! They want to take me back!" he yelled.

"That's cool, but look, I should probably head back home," I said with a false tone of urgency.

He just looked at me, puzzled. "Why are you leaving?" he asked. He turned back to the sky. "They want you to stay!"

"No, look, I should get going," I said. He grabbed my arm, and something switched inside me and bolted me away from my spot and to my car.

My hands were shaking and my heart was banging in my chest, but somehow I switched on the engine and reversed out of my driveway before he had a chance to reach me.

Brandon screamed at me to stop, so I drove faster, putting as much distance between me and him as I could. When my heart beat slowed, I switched on the radio to some loud and rebellious punk music, but the song faded and in its place was a choppy and indistinguishable high-pitched voice.

"He… he…" came from the speakers.

I tried to switch off the radio, but the volume remained unchanged. The voice dissolved into a temporary static until it spoke another slew of unintelligible words, "Ph-ph-puh-puh-puh-ha-ha."

This time, the voice didn't abate. It was a constant flow of almost-words. I tried switching off the radio again, but the words continued.

"Only five more minutes until home," I told myself.

I sped past a collection of local businesses and restaurants. The lights that lit up their display names and advertising signs were flickering on and off. Then the yellow lines on the road flickered like cars passed me by.

"Pshhhhhh—he-hel-help—pshhhhh."

"Stop! This isn't happening!" I screamed to the radio, pressing my foot harder against the gas pedal.

"Tyler! Help me!" yelled Brandon. But it wasn't through my speakers any more; his voice was in my head! I swerved across the road before desperately taking back control of the wheel. Inside my head, Brandon screamed, "They have me, Tyler! You left me alone, and they took me! Help! Help! HELP!"

Distortion from the radio was at max volume. The lights of all the local buildings were flashing faster than before, and my head kept ringing at a pitch so high that it was deafening and unbearable at the same time. "Tyler! They are going to take you! They found me! They found me! They—"

"SQRRRREEEEEEEEEEERRRRRRLLLLLKKK!"

Suddenly, everything was quiet.

I launched myself out of my still-speeding car and rolled to the side of the road. It happened so quickly that I had no clue where my body would land. There was no time to process any pain I may have felt, what became of my car, or where I was. Darkness was everywhere; it was everything. The only piece my brain eventually comprehended was my broken body flattened out on the hard surface of the road.

I couldn't move, and then Brandon's screams flooded my ears. They banged around my head, like tiny knives cutting through my eardrums, then all at once it was quiet. Everything was quiet. I couldn't even hear my own breath. But I did feel warmth trickle out of my ears, then above me came multicolored lights, moving in a circular rotation, radiating red, blue, purple, and pink. And I saw, within the lights was Brandon, a being of the sky.

(Present Day)

Nobody believes what I saw that night. Turns out I'm not so different from my old friend. I live with the same paranoia he did. Always looking over my shoulder, distrusting the media, and living in a dark room, covered with my own filth.

I've given up on trying to get my therapist to understand the truth. He doesn't get the same disdainful looks I get, or hear Brandon's screaming. He'll never truly understand until he stops trusting the media and looking up at the sky.

Maybe Brandon will be looking back at him.

Between Mimas and Tethys

Joshua G J Insole

For a while there, I thought Sirena Ryan might be invincible.

The drill slowed to a stop, the whine of machinery wound down. Somewhere beneath the iced-over ground, water sloshed. If I strained my ears, I could almost tell myself I heard it. Like the hush and shush of the waves back on Earth. Beneath the crackle and crunch of the great ice sheets upon which we stood. We all grinned at each other through our visors. For one brief moment, the minus 200 degrees Celsius didn't bother us. Neither did the rumble and shudder of the distant geysers—which made us flinch. We had made the first physical contact with alien water. We'd beaten Team Europa.

All thanks to Sirena. So, yes, I thought her immortal.

And I mean, who can blame me? She led us to the other side of the solar system and brought us out the other side in one piece. Would we have gotten even that far without her? Hard to say. The asteroid belt near Jupiter could have spelled the end for us. The woman feared nothing—neither man nor the vacuum of space. I had, if I must tell the truth, come to think of her as some sort of god. Sent down to Earth to join the mere mortals. Only to lead us off that godforsaken planet in search of something more.

To Enceladus.

One of Saturn's moons. One of its lesser moons. Over 80 objects spin around the planet, the biggest of which—Titan—outweighs Mercury. In comparison, the frozen comet Enceladus is but a mote of dust. The ice reflects so much sunlight, the climate is a perennial winter. It's a wee bit chilly, to say the least. Named after the Greek giant who revolted against Zeus, and suffered a bolt of lightning for it. They say that he lies buried beneath Mt Etna. Whenever he shifts or breaths, he causes tremors and eruptions. Having heard the rumble of Enceladus's geysers, I'm not so sure it's a myth. But they got the location of his burial wrong—by a billion kilometres or so.

The lights beneath the ice continued to dance. We still didn't know what they were—they'd surfaced soon after we'd begun to drill. But now that we'd switched the machinery off, they remained. Could be that they were some aberration of light. Could be we'd fractured some deep tectonic plate, released some pockets of gas. We'd find out, soon enough. We'd finish ground-penetrating radar within 24 hours. Lightning fast, when you took into account how long it had taken us to get there—eight years, give or take.

But not fast enough for Sirena.

"Rosa," she gestured with one gloved come hither motion.

I approached. When your captain gives you an order, you obey. When your friend asks for something, you offer your services. When the best of humanity wants a word, you damn well listen.

"Captain?" Her excitement rippled out in waves. I had a feeling that I knew what she'd say.

She didn't want to wait for *GPR* to finish. "I wanna get down there. Team Europa's almost there. They're not far behind." Her helmet shook from side to side. "I don't wanna wait. If they beat us to the punchline at this late stage, I'll fly myself right into the Sun."

Of course, the chances of Team Europa beating us into the water were slim. The last we'd heard, they'd only set up their drill and begun *GPR*. We had it. We'd won. Sirena's words were the required bluff to make it seem like the choice had left our hands. But I understood the *real* meaning. I could read between the lines. Hell, I knew her well enough. *I want to go down there now because I can. I'm like a child on Christmas Eve with a beautifully wrapped present in their hands.*

To anyone else, I—Rosalind Adkins, second in command—would have frowned. "Are you sure?" I would have asked. "It's against protocol," I would have said. But Sirena existed on a higher plateau. Her brain worked at a faster pace. She invented, analyzed, then discarded theories that would make lesser minds fracture.

"I'll see what I can do." Goddam me, that's what I said. Goddam me, and goddam the rest of the crew. Nobody asked questions. Nobody raised any voices or concerns. The excitement of discovery coursed through our veins. We had the next step in human evolution at our helm. And—of course—we all wanted to see the alien world beneath the ice. Water. Honest-to-goodness water. Who'd want to wait for some slow radar to tell us what we could find out with our own eyes?

Within the hour, we had the one-man sub prepped and the bore's drill bit pulled out. We worked in record time. Funny, isn't it? How mundane tasks take a certain length of time, but when you're nervous and feverish, time warps and ripples?

Sirena waved to us from the cockpit of the Deepsea Challenger Two, also known as *EDCV-2*. Somewhere in orbit around Jupiter, the *EDCV-1* sat, silent and still until Team Europa needed it. How would they feel, as they climbed into that claustrophobic little coffin? If I were in their shoes, I'd rather not know. But we'd have to inform them. Chances of it happening twice—on two moons in orbit around different planets—were slim to none. A distance of 734 million kilometers separated them.

A beautiful yellow cylindrical capsule, which—once in the brine—would float vertically. It looked rather odd. You'd expect it to swim with the long side horizontal, as the submarines of old did. Instead, it bobbed in the water like a sleeping sperm whale. The pilot's sphere sat at the bottom of the sub, with two utility boons on either side of the window for sample collection with the outer world.

"Camera's looking good!" said Miyake Yuudai, from the bridge of our ship. From the window, he made an okay gesture. "I can see everything you see. Absolutely crystal."

"Say something," said Kamala Narasimhan over the radio.

Sirena paused for a moment, then broke into a rather decent Elvis impression. "Uh, testing, testing, one-two-three. This is the King, can ya hear meh?"

We all grinned. "Hear you loud and clear, captain," said Kamala. "But don't be surprised if the ice causes some interference between now and then. That's perfectly normal."

"Looks like we're good to go." I crouched down

next to the sphere. Angled as the sub was, she was laid back and relaxed. We'd slide the *EDCV-2* to the lip of the bored hole. A steep incline—but not too steep—would see her down to Enceladus's ocean. Like a slip and slide.

Sirena prodded and clicked at the array of buttons, which beeped and flashed in the cockpit. "Lemme at 'em!"

Sirena tucked all the *EDCV*'s extremities in, like a passenger on a rollercoaster to prevent one of the utility boons or stabilizing fins from being knocked off on the way down.

The manned sub weighed little more than two adults. The dark hole in the ice yawned ahead, an eye from another dimension.

"Cannonball!" said Sirena.

And then the ice took her.

The yellow streak disappeared into the eternal blue. The scraping of metal against the glacier screeched. We stood at the open hole for a few moments, in awe of our achievement. We listened, watched, and waited—as if confetti would fire from the tunnel.

"C'mon, gang." I hooked a thumb over my shoulder. "Let's go watch her from inside. Don't wanna get frostbitten." Our suits could withstand a wide stretch of temperatures. Only temporarily.

We got back up on deck in time to see the last of the ice blur past Miyake's screen. Electric-blue, snow-white, ink-black. Somehow all at the same time. Splotches of brown and green, which I had a suspicion about—but didn't want to get my hopes up. But it seemed Kamala had spotted those, too.

"Look at those stains in the ice!" Her voice contained palpable joy. "Those look like microbial life!"

"Maybe, Kal," I said. "Let's not get ahead of ourselves." But, deep inside, I knew she was right. "Baby steps. We'll sample it all, in due time." I glanced up at our tech team. "Anyone see any signs of air pockets, anything that might've caused the lights?"

Miyake shook his head. "That's a negative, Rosa. But—"

Kamala jabbed a finger at the screen. "Look out! Here we go!"

We turned to the screen to see an infinite blackness race up towards the sub.

Through the audio feed came a splash. The noise told us little, but we gleaned a few titbits. The liquid shared the same viscosity as Earthbound oceans.

Heavy breathing.

Clicks and electric *bleeps* and *bloops*.

The *floodlights* thumped on and illuminated the immediate waters outside the sub.

"Oh my god," whispered Miyake.

I stared into the tenebrosity that filled our screens. Dust and fragments floated through the *EDCV*'s lights. Those little particulates looked familiar. We'd all done dives down to Mariana Trench. Nostalgia and longing washed over me.

"—ooks li—plankto—o me." Sirena's voice fuzzed in and out. Clips of words, fragments of a sentence. But we all understood.

"Yes, Sirena," said Kamala. "Looks the same to us up here. You have to get samples."

The noise that came from the sub then could be mistaken for nothing else: laughter. The sound of it made my heart warm. "All i—ue tim—amala. All—n due—ime. For now, I'm jus—ooking."

"Don't forget to place a marker," I said.

"—ust abou—to."

The hole in the ice loomed in our feeds. At its thickest, the ice grew to a layer of thirty-five kilometers.

Nigh on impenetrable.

One of the utility boons entered the frame and reached out for the ice with a robotic claw. *Ka-CHUNK*. A small red light flashed in the gloom. It crunched into the surface and embedded itself. A homeward beacon for Sirena.

"—ere you go, Rosa. —can —top—worryi—now."

I smiled at my screen. "Thanks."

"Now, —irection?"

"North," Kamala said. "North is the only sensible place to go."

"Ri—you are, Mis—Nara—han."

A low hum. A slosh of water. The camera shuddered.

"Take it nice and slow. Can always come back and look again tomorrow. Just take it easy." True. Recovering the sub from the waters would take longer than sliding down—thanks to the moon's gravity. But not a particularly difficult task, as long as we kept the hole open. If we left it too long, it'd freeze over.

In the distance, something flashed. The light flickered through the endless brine. It lit up the eternal blackness for one brief snapshot in time.

"—oly shi—. You guy—ee —at?"

Miyake and Kamala gasped. So did I.

"Is that—" I cleared my throat and spoke louder. "Is that the same light we saw from up here?"

"Look—o be."

Miyake then said the words that clanged with ominous foreshadowing. "Be careful, captain."

"Al—ays am, —yake."

Uwe Ziegler buzzed in through comms. "Uh, Rosa? Initial reports from *GPR* are in, and…"

"Yes?"

"You're gonna wanna see it. I'll let you make your own judgments. Sending them through now. Might take a few minutes."

"—m —onna turn—ights o—"

The snake in my chest squirmed and stirred and bared its fangs. It hissed and then slithered away, to hide behind the maze of bones and flesh.

The file from Uwe opened. It was incomplete data, but enough to send my heartbeat into spasms. "What—?"

The lights from the *EDCV* died, and the shadows rushed in.

On the horizon, the light took shape. A small orb that glowed in the distance. The snake in my chest whispered something. Something long-forgotten, from a crash course in marine biology.

I glanced between screens, zoomed in, bashed buttons. From the *GPR* Uwe had toiled over since we'd made base. To the black stain of the world visible through the sub's camera feed. Back to the radar mapping—with added electromagnetic snapshots. To the underwater view; the light strobed, closer now.

All at once, the pieces fell into place.

My heart tripped over itself, and the blood in my veins turned to ice. Every hair stood on end. The water evaporated from my mouth. At first, the words wouldn't come—the realization had winded me, punched me in the gut. A belt tightened around my chest. I couldn't breathe. I fought against my body and wheezed in a mouthful of the ship's recycled air. And another. And another.

And then I said the words that would come back to haunt me.

There are a million different things I should have said. Words that Sirena couldn't mishear or misconstrue. Something clearer. Something succinct and obvious. Protocol dictated the use of easy to understand phrases—no ambiguity. But in the heat of the moment, I said what came into my head. There's a chance I'm being too hard on my-self. By the time I'd understood, considered, and put it into a simple sentence, it might have already been too late.

"It's a lure!"

The others on the bridge turned to face me.

"What the…?" said Miyake.

"Oh f—" said Kamala.

The radio crackled. Feedback hummed. Static hissed.

Sirena's words fuzzed back to us, for the first time complete and clear. "It's a law? What's a law?"

A flurry of movement.

A half-yelled curse word.

The floodlights *clunked* on. In time for us to see a colossal mouthful of needle teeth. Behind the leviathan's alien eyes, there glinted a hunger, there lurked an intelli-gence. From the space between and above, an extended protrusion dangled—a fisherman's rod. The tip of the filament glowed, luminescent: a lure.

Sirena gasped.

The creature lunged.

Her vitals spiked.

An alarm blared red.

Blurred motion outside the camera.

Bubbles frothed, water thrashed, a toothy maw gaped.

A short scream sliced short.

The feed died, cut to darkness.

Flatline.

"Sirena?" Miyake's voice. "Dammit, answer me!"

But she wouldn't.

She died on that small moon, in orbit between Mi-mas and Tethys.

Enceladus.

It twirls around Saturn, an iced-over piece of rock. Its liquid inner guts slosh and froth, and—on occasion—spill forth through cracks in the crust. Enceladus vomits

its icy vapor out for miles.
      And in the brine beneath, the monsters glide.
      All eyes turned to me, hollow in their sockets, dark against pallid countenances.

Please Pay Upon Checkout

Nikki Brooke

Everything was black. Actually, that's not accurate; everything was void of color. There was nothing, no black, just empty space. No light, no smells, no sound.

And there was no creak in her neck. No ache in her back. In fact, she had no body.

She only had her consciousness; as she slowly became aware of the nothing.

She couldn't see anything, but not because her eyes were closed; she had no eyes. She knew it, but it didn't alarm her. Instinctively, she knew she didn't possess the body she once did. She left it behind.

There was something in the emptiness, the softest breath of light, not bright enough to make her squint.

The emptiness faded. Instead of nothing, there was blackness. And in the blackness, there was a shard of light, a curve of something like sunshine reflected and glinted.

A hint of green came into focus. The black faded further, like clouds parting; beams of sunshine spilled down on the scene in front of her. The white of it blinded her.

Her mind's eye blinked, fluttering against the luster.

As if the dawn of time had awoken the day, the last of the emptiness and blackness disappeared, presenting a plentiful garden.

Sunshine glinted off the curves of lush green leaves; apricots grew plump, shining yellow; grass shimmered in shades of green and silver.

She took a deep breath and smelled the sweetness in the air, the scent of the forest, the sharpness of the grass.

Then the birds began to sing. Long sweet melodies, all in harmony.

The sense of touch came back to her, not to her physical body which was left in the real world, but as an extension of her mind. She could feel the coolness of the grass, and the warmth of the sunshine, a soft breeze, even though it had no cheek to brush.

As her senses returned, so did her memories.

Her name was Margaret.

Margaret remembered her life, not a happy one, but at least a happy ending. She'd never loved so fiercely as she had in her last weeks. When her body had already failed her, creaking and groaning when she moved, causing pain in every waking moment, her mind had still been the reliable companion it had always been. And it recognised a mind of equal measure in another; a man who could challenge and inspire her, could love and be loved, could forever keep her entranced and interested in this heavenly afterlife.

Where is Reggie, anyway?

* * *

"My name is Reginald Clark."

"Welcome to the Brickbird Consciousness Center, Mr Clark."

The receptionist behind the counter was a young man, with a full head of hair and his whole life ahead of him. Reggie didn't begrudge him this fact, not when he was about to shed his aged, mottled skin and enter the garden he and Margaret had chosen to spend their afterlife.

He wasn't sad to be ridding himself of his broken old body, with bones that rubbed together and muscles that ached. He could no longer trek mountains or dance the night away; life was much more boring than it once was.

Although he had never considered throwing away his life before it had come to a natural end, he couldn't wait a moment longer to start his afterlife with Margaret. For her, it was worth it. And he knew he didn't have very long anyway, not the way his body stopped and stuttered these days.

"I'm here to checkout," Reggie said.

* * *

The digital-heaven was even more beautiful than Margaret had imagined. The creators had made every blade of grass and every delicate leaf perfectly. Each glistened in the sun, just the right amount.

It was even more lovely than the lake she loved as a child, where she had galloped and played, charging down the slopes of the green hills and diving into the water. She giggled at the memory.

She jolted at the sound of the musical giggle. It was hers, but not hers. It sounded like the giggle she had as a young girl, not the old crone she had become.

"But you're not an old crone anymore," Margaret said to herself, relishing the youthful voice that came out, not choked by agedness.

She followed a path that weaved through the trees. There were the sounds of footsteps crunching on the gravel, even though she had no feet. She smiled, pleased with the effort and attention to detail entered into the design; it was worth every penny.

She turned a corner and the trees opened up to a crystal-clear lake, the distant mountains reflecting on its surface.

Margaret lowered herself to the ground, or at least her vision lowered, to a position somewhat like sitting cross-legged, as she might have as a child. She gazed out on the calm waters and noticed the same tranquillity within her.

She wished Reggie would hurry up and join her. He would love this place.

It would have been nice to meet Reggie when he was a young man. He has told Margaret of his adventures across the Andes; how she wished she could have been there with him. They would have had a happy life together, so suited that they were.

But not only had they not met until they were both old and grey, Reggie hadn't been free to pursue a relationship with Margaret, as much as he had wanted to. He was a married man, and too respectable to carry on behind his wife's back. And Margaret would not have been content to be the other woman.

So no, there was no chance for them to have a whirlwind romance in life, but in death, they can be together forever.

After a time, she wondered how long she had been waiting. The sun had moved across the sky, but in this simulated world there was no telling if the sun moved at the same speed as in real life. *But surely Reggie should be here by now*, Margaret thought, *maybe there is something wrong?*

She brushed the thought aside, along with visions of Reggie returning to his wife. Impossible, their life together had ended, he swore to Margaret he would join her in the afterlife.

But the thought niggled at her. Reggie had always been bound by duty; what if he felt his duty to his wife extended beyond death?

* * *

"If you can just fill in this form, please," the young man pointed to the holo projected across the counter.

Reggie's hands shook as he ticked boxes and typed out his answers. The trembling wasn't just due to his age, but also to the adrenaline that pumped through his veins.

The parting with his wife had not gone well, and it had left him a little shaken. She had screamed at him, called him a *whore, a cheat, a nasty little man.* She believed that their marriage vows should be upheld, even in death. He argued that he had only vowed to be true to her while his heart still beat.

His wife had expected him to spend his afterlife with her. "Why?" he had shouted back, "When you hate me so much?"

She had thrown her shoe at him then. It narrowly missed hitting him in the head, and he had left without another word.

Still, he did feel some duty to her. That's why he had left her all his money; he bequeathed every cent to her, not keeping anything for himself. He wouldn't need it. Margaret had enough money for both of them. She had already paid for his fare into their paradise.

* * *

Margaret walked along the pier. Through the surface of the glassy water, she spied orange fish darting between the pebbles; a nice touch to this picturesque world.

A sigh escaped her lips. *When is Reggie going to get here so we can start our afterlife together; start exploring this world properly; start exploring each other?*

She turned from the pretty view in frustration, only to be beaten by the beautiful view behind her. The challenging cliff, with its face inviting Margaret to climb it. It was as if she could feel her fingers itching and tingling with the sensation of gripping rocks as she scaled up the cliff face. A vivid memory.

She wanted so badly to start her adventures, but she wouldn't without Reggie.

He definitely should be here by now.

He wouldn't return to his wife. He wouldn't. He may have felt a duty to her in life, but their vows only hold "until death do they part." Not beyond. Reggie knew that. And he had lived his life with *Her*. He had been faithful. He had given everything to her, his ninety-six years, his body, and his happiness. Now he wished to be happy too.

No, he would not have gone back to her.

Then he must have gone senile, the thought plunged Margaret into an ocean of horror. He had been showing the signs. The more frequent memory loss, confusing meeting times and places. Maybe it was more serious than Margaret had given credit. What if he had forgotten how to get to the Brickbird Consciousness Center or forgotten about their pledge all together!

Fear paralysed Margaret and she stopped on the pier, staring at the cliffs looming over her. They no longer looked so inviting.

* * *

Completing the form with a flick on the holo, Reggie turned back to the receptionist.

"Fantastic," the receptionist gave it a cursory glance. "Take this," he said, and handed over a small vial of liquid, "Your body will begin to die within an hour of taking it, leaving your brain active and ready for transmitting."

"Do I take it now?" Reggie said, eyeing the innocent looking liquid.

The receptionist shrugged. "The sooner you take it, the sooner you'll reach your digital-heaven." Reggie downed the liquid.

"Right. While we're waiting for that to take effect, I'll finalise your forms for your checkout." The receptionist didn't offer any condolences for the loss of life, or any comforting words for what is to become of Reggie, but turned promptly back to his screen.

Reggie looked around, not knowing what to do with himself. He saw a chair, and with no other instructions, went to sit down.

"Wait a moment," the receptionist said. Reggie stopped midway to the chair and turned back. The receptionist frowned. "Is there a problem?" Reggie asked.

"You've ticked that your fare has been prepaid, but we don't have a record of payment from you," the receptionist explained. He displayed the holo form again for Reggie to see, "You need to fill in your bank details so we can take payment."

Reggie frowned. "No," he said, trying to stay calm, "it has been paid. And besides, I have already bequeathed all my money away. I don't have a cent to my name."

"Oh," the holo went dark and the frown deepened on the receptionist's face. His eyes darted back and forth from his screen to Reggie. "Oh, my." The receptionist shook his head. "No, there is definitely no payment for you."

"There must be!" Reggie's voice was raised, and so was his heart rate. He could already feel his body shutting down. "Look again."

* * *

Margaret was halfway around the lake. The place was too silent without the distraction of people and responsibilities.

The sun sparkled off the water as it continued to lower. The sky changed with pinks and oranges melting into dark blue.

She missed the way Reggie would light up when he saw her, a big silly grin spreading across his creased and aged face. How they would talk for hours about books or movies, world politics, and current affairs. How he would make her laugh, just by being him.

She hiccupped a sob, even though she had no lungs to breath with.

What will happen to him if he has gone senile? He will be moved into the aged-care facility, monitored day and night by nurses until the day he dies. His belongings will go to his wife.

She stopped. A thought nagged at her.

If he was classified as senile, his last will and testament would be read. And his will stated his desire to enter the afterlife with Margaret. Even if his body could no longer process his thoughts, his mind would still function in the afterlife with the high capacity of the processors Margaret had paid for.

She would just have to wait until he was brought to the consciousness center and they would be reunited once again.

* * *

Reggie paced up and down the reception room to stay alert. He knew he would never wake up if he fell asleep. But before long, his legs couldn't hold him up any longer. He fell into one of the seats.

The receptionist had looked for the funds repeatedly. But it was no use, the money wasn't there, it had somehow been lost in transmission.

Reggie had insisted on speaking to the manager, but they hadn't arrived yet.

Slowly the edges of his vision faded to white. His toes and fingers tingled and then lost all feeling. His body slumped further in the chair. His mind pushed at the sleep, trying to find a solution, but it was like swimming through custard. It was no use. There was no fighting it.

His thoughts turned to Margaret. Her bright mind and intelligence. He would miss her.

The whiteness at the edge of his vision grew like a thick mist and obliterated his sight. There was nothing. Just one last breath and then Reggie was gone.

* * *

Margaret waited patiently for days and weeks. Several months passed and she still waited, but her hopes diminished with each hour. She knew now he wasn't coming. She knew she had to endure this perfect digital-heaven alone.

She'd been alone her whole life, she wasn't scared of doing it in the afterlife too. But she was disappointed. And she missed Reggie.

He must have gone back to his wife, she thought, and her heart broke, never to be put back together again.

Author Bios

Elizabeth Suggs

Elizabeth Suggs is the founder of the LUW Romance Writers Chapter, co-owner of the indie publisher Collective Tales Publishing, owner of Editing Mee, and is the author of a growing number of published stories, two of which were in a podcast and poetry journal. She is a book reviewer (EditingMee.com) and popular bookstagramer and cosplayer (@ElizabethSuggsAuthor). When she's not writing or reading, she's playing video and board games or making cookies.

Jonathan Reddoch

*Jonathan Reddoch is co-owner of Collective Tales Publishing. He is a father, writer, editor, and publisher. He writes sci-fi, fantasy, romance, and especially horror. He has been working on his enormous sci-fi novel for over a decade and would like to finish it in this lifetime if possible. Find him on Instagram: Allusions_of_Grandeur_*

Katie Collupy
Katie Collupy is the author of Blood Voyager, *a sweeping science fiction crime novel. While being a writer, she is also a dedicated student who is passionate about the pursuit of justice. She received her Bachelor's of Arts in Criminal Justice from Florida Atlantic University. When she's not writing creatively or academically, she can be found wandering through the wilderness in search of the next best sunset.*

Brenda Radchik
Brenda is a Mexican author with a BA in International Relations. She also has a diploma from Oxford University for the Online Advanced Creative Writing Course Currently and is working on a sci-fi novel while enrolled in the Certificate for Creative Writing at UCSD.
Twitter: Radchik_1313 Instagram: @Brendaradchikwrites

Nikki Brooke
Nikki Brooke grew up in Australia but instead of spending time riding on the backs of kangaroos (which is not recommended), she spent it with her head in books. She's a self-proclaimed geek, loving science fiction, fantasy, history and mythology and is proud of it— which is probably obvious since she's a science fiction and fantasy writer, and she named her dogs, Osiris and Apollo, after ancient gods.

AR Mirabal
A R Mirabal is a science fiction fantasy author & artist as well as podcast host of The A.R.T. Podcast where he promotes fellow creatives and talk about the creative process. He was born in Dominican Republic, and has lived in many different places since then. He currently live near Boston and has two doggos—Paco & Nebula. His debut novel, Allegory of the End *(Volume One), came out last year on the Summer solstice and signed*

copies with merch/bookmarks/posters related to the story will be available at the start of January.

Patrick Moody
Patrick Moody is the author of The Gravedigger's Son *and* Creatures of Clay. *His short fiction has appeared in* Lovecraft in a Time of Madness, A Monster Told Me Bedtime Stories *(Monsters Vol. 7),* Dark Moon Digest *and also has been adapted on* The Wicked Library *and* Campfire Radio Theater. *He and his wife live outside New Haven, Connecticut.*

Alex Child
Writing has a unique power, and Alex Child is just smart enough to know that he's nowhere near smart enough to accurately describe it. Between working half as hard as he should and twice as hard as required at his day job, he continues pursuing that indescribable emotional swell from relating to a literary character and sharing their experiences. He hopes his story brings you even just a portion of that rush.

D A Butcher
He is half British, half Italian, and grew up in London, England. He worked as a comic and movie journalist for three years, voluntarily, to refine his writing skills. He has won writing competitions for his short-stories and poetry, and been shortlisted for others in leading writing magazines. He recently had a short-story placed in a digital anthology. He now lives in the Midlands, UK, with his wife and three children. Dylan is studying towards his Master's Degree in English Literature and Creative Writing with the Open University, and dreams of becoming a commercially successful author. He recently self-published his debut novel, Eyes of Sleeping Children, *which is available to buy on Amazon.*

Virginia Babcock
Virginia Babcock has always loved romantic fiction, and now writes her own stories of love and life in the real world and beyond. Virginia lives in Missouri where she works full-time when she's not writing books. Her husband and cat keep her constantly entertained the rest of the time.

Joshua Insole
Three-time Reedsy winner Joshua G. J. Insole is a British writer who lives in the Austrian Alps. Author of several other shortlisted stories, he published his first book in 2020. Joshua's favoured genres are horror and science fiction.

Matthew A. Goodwin
Matthew A. Goodwin has been writing about space-ships, dragons, and adventures since he was a child. After creating his first fantasy world at twelve years old, he never stopped writing. Storytelling happened only in the background for over a decade as he spent his days caring for wildlife as a zookeeper, but when his son was born, he decided to pursue his lifelong dream of becoming an author. Having always loved sweeping space operas and gritty cyberpunk stories that asked questions about man's relationship to technology, he penned the international bestselling series, A Cyberpunk Saga. *His passion for the genre also inspired him to create and co-found Cyberpunk Day ™, a celebration of all things high tech / low life in the arts. He is now expanding his science fiction universe into space. For more information and free content, visit* https://www.thutoworld.com/

Want more?

Check out our current and future anthologies at
www.CTPFiction.com